"You can*not* be serious." Tilly was incredulous. **"You're actually offering to come home with me for Christmas and pretend to be my boyfriend?"**

"We could make it work," he said. "It might even be fun. What do you say?"

Harry's smile stretched into a cheeky grin. It made Tilly imagine what this man had been like as a kid. A happy, mischievous little boy who probably got away with almost anything because he'd been born with the ability to charm those around him and make the world feel like a better place.

Her father deserved to feel like that. Especially at Christmastime.

A tiny shiver ran down Tilly's spine as she thought of that heat Harry had conjured up from nowhere with just the touch of his hands and the tone of his voice. And for a heartbeat, it had made Tilly remember a time when she'd believed that dreams could come true.

And…maybe it would be nice to feel like that again. Even if it was just a pretense. Even if it was only for Christmas.

"I'll think about it,"

Dear Reader,

My family always went on our annual summer camping holiday to Central Otago in the South Island of New Zealand just after Christmas, so there's a very strong connection for me between the seasonal celebrations and this favorite part of my country. I have, however, been lucky enough to have spent many Christmases on the other side of the world, and (just whispering here) I secretly prefer a winter Christmas, so I have great sympathy for my hero in *The Doctor's Christmas Homecoming*, Harry, who thinks that Christmas in the middle of summer is totally wrong.

Harry can't wait to get back to his native Ireland to try to find what's missing from his life, but he's in for a very unexpected change of heart when he finds himself in Tilly's world in Central Otago, where you can get sunburned on Christmas Day but traditions are strangely familiar and the real spirit of Christmas is all around you.

Merry Christmas, Kiwi-style! I very much hope that this story is a small extra gift for you.

With love,

Alison xx

THE DOCTOR'S CHRISTMAS HOMECOMING

———

ALISON ROBERTS

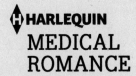

HARLEQUIN
MEDICAL
ROMANCE

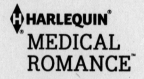

HARLEQUIN®
MEDICAL
ROMANCE™

Recycling programs
for this product may
not exist in your area.

ISBN-13: 978-1-335-73746-5

The Doctor's Christmas Homecoming

Copyright © 2022 by Alison Roberts

For questions and comments about the quality of this book,
please contact us at CustomerService@Harlequin.com.

Harlequin Enterprises ULC
22 Adelaide St. West, 41st Floor
Toronto, Ontario M5H 4E3, Canada
www.Harlequin.com

Printed in U.S.A.

Alison Roberts has been lucky enough to live in the south of France for several years recently but is now back in her home country of New Zealand. She is also lucky enough to write for the Harlequin Medical Romance line. A primary school teacher in a former life, she later became a qualified paramedic. She loves to travel and dance, drink champagne, and spend time with her daughter and her friends. Alison Roberts is the author of over one hundred books!

Books by Alison Roberts

Harlequin Medical Romance

Two Tails Animal Refuge
The Vet's Unexpected Family

Royal Christmas at Seattle General
Falling for the Secret Prince

Unlocking the Rebel's Heart
Stolen Nights with the Single Dad
Christmas Miracle at the Castle
Miracle Baby, Miracle Family
A Paramedic to Change Her Life
One Weekend in Prague

Visit the Author Profile page
at Harlequin.com for more titles.

**Praise for
Alison Roberts**

"Ms. Roberts has delivered a delightful read in this book where the chemistry between this couple was strong from the moment they meet… The romance was heart-warming."

—*Harlequin Junkie* on
Melting the Trauma Doc's Heart

CHAPTER ONE

'THAT SHOULDN'T HAVE HAPPENED. It was so unprofessional. I'm really sorry…'

Big blue eyes were filling with tears and Dr Matilda Dawson felt her heart sink another notch as she pulled a handful of tissues from the box and held them out. Night shift in a busy big city emergency department could be a challenge at any time. In the final run-up to Christmas, at the peak of silly season, it could be absolute chaos.

Everything had been under control until now—apart from having been unable to return a second missed call from her father, which was enough to make Tilly wonder if something had gone wrong with the plan for her to spend Christmas Day with her only family member. An opportunity to make a quick call had been ambushed, however, when Tilly had observed a junior nurse struggling to cope with the relatively simple task of taking an ECG on a patient who'd come in with chest pain.

Tilly had had no choice but to divert another nurse to do the ECG and whisk a clearly very unhappy young staff member into this office space to find out what the problem was. They couldn't afford to have people on the front line who were distracted enough to be unable to function efficiently.

'I'll pull myself together.' The nurse, Charlotte, blew her nose and then sniffed decisively. 'Honestly, this is stupid. I'm twenty-one. It's not as if I haven't been dumped before but...'

Oh, no... Tilly could see someone over Charlotte's shoulder, walking past the open door of this office. Someone who was smiling at her. The someone who'd apparently just broken Charlotte's heart.

'Merry almost Christmas,' he said, in that adorable Irish accent that would have captured any woman's attention if, inexplicably, the smile hadn't already done the trick.

Tilly glared at him. This is *your* fault, was the silent message. You should be ashamed of yourself, Harry Doyle.

'This is entirely *my* fault,' Charlotte said,

as if Tilly had spoken aloud. Her voice was wobbling as she turned her head to see Harry's back. 'He told me, right from the start. He said he'd go to the concert I had an extra ticket for but it would only be as a friend. It wasn't a date or anything. But it *felt* like a date… And I really thought he might be the *one*…you know?'

'Yeah…' Tilly's tone was a little grim. She knew. 'Why did it feel like a date?' she asked cautiously. 'He didn't try and—'

'Oh, no,' Charlotte said hurriedly, shaking her head. 'Not at all. He didn't even try to kiss me goodnight afterwards.'

She sounded deeply disappointed and Tilly felt suddenly weary. Was Charlotte so innocent she didn't realise that making herself so available could have had a very different outcome? One that could haunt her for years to come?

'You must have been aware that he's been out with almost every single woman in this hospital, and that's quite an achievement when he's only been here for a few months.'

Okay, so that was a bit of an exaggeration, but Tilly had had him pegged from the moment she'd been introduced to him and had been the recipient of *that* smile, along with a gleam that could only be described as flirtatious in those distinctive, smoky grey-blue eyes. Harry Doyle might have come with very good professional references but, on a personal level, he was a player. A good-looking Irish rogue who could use his not inconsiderable charm to rule the world and everyone in it.

Apart from Tilly, of course.

'I know. But then you think that it might be different this time. That you might be the one *they've* been looking for all along.' Charlotte took a deep breath. 'Sorry,' she said again. 'I'm fine, really. It won't be a problem. I need to get back to my patients.'

Tilly could see her scanning the department as they walked towards the central hub. Bright red and green cardboard letters stuck to the front of the desk welcomed patients with the seasonal Maori greeting of *Meri Kirihimete* and there was a tiny, unobtrusive Christmas tree on one end of the counter, wrapped in silver tinsel with a star on top. There were two ambulance crews waiting for the triage nurse to decide where the new patients could go and some junior doctors and medical students were focused on computer screens to check past medical records or look for X-ray or laboratory results.

A cleaner, wearing a cheerful Santa hat, was mopping the floor nearby and a technician was humming a Christmas carol as he pushed a trolley past. Tilly could see that Harry was standing beside the patient who'd required the detailed ECG as part of the process of investigating whether his chest pain might be a symptom of a heart attack.

Charlotte had seen Harry as well and Tilly could almost feel her brushing off her earlier despair. She was smiling now. Almost beaming, in fact, as she caught Tilly's gaze.

'It's Christmas,' she said, as if she realised her dramatic mood change might need an explanation. 'And you never know… Miracles *can* happen.'

Harry could see Charlotte coming towards him from the corner of his eye but he didn't look away from his patient.

'Can you describe this pain for me?'

'It was like being kicked by a horse. Right here.' The man put his hand over the left side of his chest.

'So it came on suddenly? What were you doing?'

'I had a crate of beer in the basement. Couple of dozen. I was bringing them in to put in the fridge because we've got a barbecue tomorrow, but I had to stop when I was only halfway up the steps. I couldn't breathe, Doc, and then it hit me. *Wham…* My missus had to call an ambulance because I couldn't move, the pain was so bad I felt sick and I got all sweaty, but they got there really fast.'

Harry nodded. Telling the emergency services that a middle-aged man had severe chest pain, nausea and sweating *would* get an ambulance on the way very quickly. The paramedics had taken an ECG that was normal, however, and a repeat one done when he'd arrived in the department didn't show any abnormalities. The patient report form the paramedic team had completed stated no medical history of any cardiac or other major health problems either.

Charlotte came into the cubicle with an apologetic smile. 'I'm so sorry I had to dash off like that, Gerald,' she said. 'But I'm back now and I'm going to take very good care of you.'

'Thanks, darlin'.' Gerald was grinning at the pretty blonde nurse. 'I'm feeling better already.'

His smile vanished, however, when Harry put his hands on his chest wall to examine him. '*Ouch*...that really hurts.'

Harry could feel Charlotte's gaze on him. She was poised to follow any direction he might give to administer painkillers. Or to deal with a cardiac arrest? She was so young and eager. And it was disconcertingly obvious that she had a bit of a crush on him.

'Can you take a deep breath?' he asked Gerald.

The intake of breath was interrupted by a sharp groan.

'Too painful?'

Gerald nodded, his face still crumpled in agony. Charlotte put her hand on his shoulder. 'It's okay,' she told him. 'We're going to look after you.'

'It might not feel like it, but it's good news that the pain gets worse with a deep breath,' Harry said. 'Along with your normal test results, we can be confident that you're not having the heart attack you thought you were having. You've pulled one of your intercostal muscles—the ones that go between your ribs and make up the chest wall. It'll be sore for a few days so you'll need to avoid any strenuous activity. I'll write you a script for some anti-inflammatories.'

He could feel Charlotte's gaze following him as he went to print out a prescription and sign a discharge summary. 'You were lucky enough to get the best doctor we've got,' he heard her tell Gerald. 'Isn't he wonderful?'

Tilly Dawson didn't think so. She was glaring at him as he paused by the central desk to deal with his paperwork. She hadn't been that thrilled to see him when he'd greeted her earlier, come to think of it. Was it because he was filling in for a friend and she hadn't expected to have to work with him? Or was it just that, for some reason, she really didn't like him? He'd long since given up trying to charm this colleague and, given her cool, controlled demeanour, he hadn't been surprised to discover she had the nickname of being the 'Ice Queen'. They had managed to avoid working closely together so far but he'd been in this department at the same time often enough and he couldn't remember ever seeing Matilda Dawson smile with any real warmth. Or hearing her laugh, come to think of it.

Somehow, her lack of friendliness seemed more undeserved tonight. It was only a couple of days until Christmas, for heaven's sake—the universal time for goodwill and kindness—and they had the rest of a night shift to get through together. It was after midnight already and he could hear a very inebriated patient shouting from one end of the department, a small child shrieking from another corner and there was more than one phone ringing. A flashing light was a signal that a radio call needed to be answered from an incoming ambulance, which usually meant that a serious case was on the way. It was shaping up to be a long night and Harry did not need any extra tension from feeling like he'd done something wrong.

So he smiled at Tilly. One of his best smiles. 'How's it going?'

She didn't smile back. 'It's fine,' she said. 'Or it will be, if you don't upset any more of our nurses.'

Harry's smile evaporated. 'I have no idea what you're talking about.'

Except…she'd been talking to Charlotte when he'd walked past earlier and the young nurse had been clutching a handful of tissues. He'd wondered at the time if Charlotte had been upset by a patient death or that perhaps she was being reprimanded for a failure to follow a strict protocol that he could be sure Tilly would have spotted instantly, but maybe he'd been miles off the mark.

And maybe it had been a bad idea to go to that concert the other evening, but Charlotte had told him it was a departmental group outing that she just happened to have an extra ticket for. He'd thought it was odd they hadn't come across anyone they knew in the mosh pit, but the music and dancing had been great fun and he'd made it crystal clear before he'd accepted that invitation and again at the end of the evening that it hadn't been any kind of a date. Hadn't he?

If Tilly could see his silent question, she wasn't about to answer it. She simply turned away to speak to the nurse who had picked up the ambulance call.

'Post cardiac arrest case en route,' he heard the nurse say. 'ETA three minutes. Fifty-six-year-old male who's in sinus bradycardia but still being ventilated. I'll get the catheter lab on standby.'

Harry looked at the growing list of patients that had been allocated to him. The sore throat in one of the curtained cubicles had been waiting a while now. He picked up the patient file from the desk as Tilly moved swiftly away towards a resuscitation area where she would be continuing treatment for someone lucky enough to have beaten the odds and survived a cardiac arrest. So far. Way more exciting than a sore throat, that was for sure.

Not that he was going to waste any mental energy feeling envious of others having a more interesting challenge. Or feeling hard done by because someone disliked him for no obvious reason. It reminded him of some of the more miserable moments of his childhood, when he'd had to change schools as his mother moved them yet again in search of a cheaper rental or a better job. He might have learned that making people laugh or feel good was a quick way to make friends but he'd also learned that there were some people who weren't going to like you no matter how hard you tried and it didn't really matter because you could just move on and make a fresh start.

Harry Doyle was thirty-six and he'd lost count of the number of fresh starts he'd made in his life so far. He'd been in New Zealand for a good three months now but, as much as he loved the country and its people, it felt increasingly as if there was something missing from his life. It might already be time to think about moving on again.

Somewhere a bit closer to home, he decided as he introduced himself to an eighteen-year-old who had come to the city to spend Christmas with friends. It looked as if Talia had come from a summer beach party with the shorts she was wearing along with an oversized singlet over a bikini top. Harry added a condition to that decision to move on before he pushed it aside to focus on his patient. His next destination needed to be back in the northern hemisphere. Celebrating Christmas in the middle of summer felt so wrong it might be a big part of the reason he was feeling as if something needed fixing in his life.

Something was also clearly wrong with the throat he found himself peering at moments later. The ominous spots on the red and swollen tissue of the throat and tonsils, combined with the fever and painfully enlarged lymph nodes of his patient suggested a strep infection and, with a young Pasifika patient, he knew the risk was greater of it becoming something more serious like rheumatic fever. Starting antibiotics had to be a priority.

'We'll do a rapid antigen test for strep throat, Talia. If it's positive we'll start you on a ten-day course of antibiotics. Are you allergic to any medications, like penicillin?'

Talia shook her head. 'Don't think so.'

'Have you got a nurse looking after you?'

She nodded this time. 'She went to find me an ice block. She said it might help make it easier to swallow.'

It was Charlotte who arrived with the fruit-flavoured frozen snack. Her face lit up when she saw Harry.

'I was just looking for you,' she exclaimed. 'Gerald's waiting for his discharge form so he can go home. Someone else was asking where you were too.' She smiled at him. 'You're popular tonight.'

Popularity wasn't Harry's goal. He would be happy to settle for being able to keep all the balls he was juggling up in the air without dropping any of them. He had a patient with severe abdominal pain that could be appendicitis. Or a kidney stone. Or possibly a urinary tract infection, but she'd been unable to provide a sample for analysis. She was due back from a CT scan but Harry needed to find the swab for Talia's rapid antigen test and check on the diabetic patient from earlier in the night who was being observed as he recovered from a hypoglycaemic episode. When Talia's test result was positive for strep throat, he went back to let her know.

'You can have a one-off injection of penicillin,' he told her. 'If that's preferable to taking a ten-day course of pills twice a day. It's very important that you don't miss any doses with the pills or stop them in a few days because you're feeling better. This bug can come back or hang around and cause other problems down the track. It can even damage the valves in your heart, which can be very serious.'

'I'm going camping for Christmas with my friends.' Talia bit her lip. 'So it might be difficult to remember to take pills. Is the injection really painful?'

'It's got local anaesthetic in with it, so it's not too bad,' Harry promised. 'Then you just need to wait here for twenty minutes or so to make sure you don't have any kind of allergic reaction.'

Harry was thinking about Talia's planned trip as he headed for the drug room to prepare her medication. It was another weird thing about this side of the world, wasn't it?

He'd heard that some New Zealand camping grounds were magnets to celebrate Christmas or see in the New Year in the sun, preferably beside a beach or a lake, but he could remember how excited he'd been as a kid when it started snowing in time for the big day. He still had a photograph somewhere of him and his mother standing beside the best snowman in the world that they'd created.

'Are your friends going to take you home?' he asked Talia.

'Yes. They got sick of waiting so they went to get hamburgers.'

'I'd like to talk to them before you go. About being careful with sharing food and drinks while you're camping and that they'll need to see a doctor if they get any symptoms themselves.'

When Harry came out of Talia's cubicle having administered the injection, he saw a patient being wheeled out of Resus with a medical team surrounding the bed that included the senior consultant on duty. If it was the same one who'd been rushed in, the change was astonishing. He wasn't being ventilated any longer. He wasn't unconscious. Propped up on pillows, the middle-aged man was awake. Smiling, even.

Harry veered towards Resus as Tilly emerged. 'Is that the post-cardiac arrest guy?'

Tilly nodded. 'He's finally stable enough to be on his way to the cath lab for angioplasty.'

Managing the critically ill patient had obviously been a challenge. Tilly's cheeks were pink and there was a strand of long dark hair that had managed to work itself loose from the tight braid she always wore. He could sense her satisfaction in the case and he knew what that felt like. He could feel a corner of his mouth lift in a wry smile. Dr Matilda might not like him very much but they had something quite significant in common, didn't they?

'Well done,' he said quietly. 'He's a lucky man.'

'He's had a massive left anterior STEMI so he's not out of the woods yet.' Tilly was scanning the department as if she was trying to decide where she might be most needed next. An ambulance stretcher was being rushed into the second resuscitation area beside them, where the trauma team being led by the HOD was waiting. That could mean there were other patients who'd been temporarily abandoned so that the incoming emergency could be dealt with. The whole department was on a knife-edge that could tip them into chaos at any moment.

And Tilly was frowning. 'Oh, no...' she muttered. 'What's wrong *this* time?'

Harry followed her line of sight to see Charlotte rushing out of the cubicle he'd been in only minutes ago, to administer Talia's injection. And something *was* very clearly wrong. Charlotte looked absolutely terrified.

'Help!' she called. 'Someone? I need help...'

Tilly followed Harry.

She'd been about to confirm she wasn't needed by the trauma team before focusing on whatever priority was deemed most urgent elsewhere in the department but Harry's reaction to spotting Charlotte trumped any other option. He *knew* something bad was happening—she could feel it by the sudden tension in his body language. No, it was more than tension. It felt like fear...

Any opinion that his reaction was a bit over the top vanished as Tilly stepped into the cubicle. A young girl was sitting bolt upright on the bed looking even more frightened than Charlotte. Her eyes were puffy and a rash was making the skin on her arms look oddly lumpy. More alarmingly, the high-pitched sound she was making as she sucked in each breath told them that there was a potentially life-threatening problem with her airway.

'Talia had intramuscular penicillin about five minutes ago,' Harry said tersely. He stomped on the brake at the end of the bed and started pushing it. Charlotte leapt out of the way, pulling the curtain open at the same time. 'Resus One's clear, isn't it?'

Harry didn't wait for Tilly's affirmative response. The area might not have been cleaned yet, with the last critically ill patient having only just been transferred, but it would have everything they could need in the way of equipment and drugs available for a respiratory emergency.

Everything except perhaps assistance at the level of skill that could be required. Tilly could see more staff rushing into Resus Two and caught a glimpse of what looked like a traumatic cardiac arrest being managed in there. The bedside space was already crowded so it was a no-brainer for Tilly to stay with Harry. She might have heard good things about his professional abilities, but she'd never worked closely with him personally and there could be a young girl's life hanging in the balance with what appeared to be an anaphylactic reaction to antibiotics unfolding in front of them.

Harry went straight to the drug cupboard in Resus One to draw up adrenaline.

'Can you get some high-flow oxygen on, please, Charlotte?' he directed. 'And we'll need the IV trolley. Tilly, could you get some ECG dots on and a set of vital signs?'

Tilly worked fast, sticking electrodes onto Talia's shoulders and abdomen so that they could monitor her heart rate and rhythm. She wrapped a blood pressure cuff around her upper arm to enable automatic measurements and clipped a pulse oximeter to her finger. She could feel her own heart rate increasing as the figures started appearing on the screen of the monitoring equipment.

'Heart rate's one thirty-two,' she relayed to Harry. 'Blood pressure's eighty-six on fifty, respirations twenty-eight and pulse ox ninety-four percent.'

In other words, her heart rate was too high, the blood pressure was too low and, despite rapid breathing, there was not enough oxygen circulating in Talia's blood, but Harry's words to their patient were as calm and reassuring as if this was nothing to be overly concerned about.

'I'm going to give you an injection in your leg,' he told her. 'It should start to help your breathing very soon. I know this is scary, Talia, but hang in there. We've got this, okay?'

Talia nodded. Charlotte, her hands shaking, was trying to fit an oxygen mask over Talia's face at the same time Harry was injecting the adrenaline into the muscle of her thigh.

'Let's find a non-rebreather mask instead of this one,' Tilly said calmly, taking the mask from Charlotte's hands. 'And we need to turn the rate up as high as possible.' She caught Harry's glance and the flash of appreciation that she was here and he wasn't having to deal with an emergency with an inexperienced and extremely nervous young nurse.

'Could you set up for a fluid challenge?' he asked. 'I'll get some IV access.'

Tilly found and checked a bag of IV fluid, hung it up and then opened a set of tubing and flow control to get it ready to attach to both the bag and an IV cannula. There was also a pressure infusion cuff that needed to be wrapped around the bag to enable rapid delivery to counteract the hypovolaemia that anaphylactic shock could cause. She was watching what Harry was doing from the corner of her eye at the same time. The combination of urticaria, dark skin and low blood pressure would make it a challenge to find a vein, let alone slip a wide-bore plastic cannula into place but, again, Harry gave the impression of being calm and confident, so Tilly wasn't surprised that he completed the procedure within seconds. She was, however, impressed enough to nod at him.

'Well done,' she murmured.

The few minutes it took to accomplish these first steps meant that it was time for a second dose of adrenaline. Judging by how little response there had been to the first dose, Tilly wondered if Harry was thinking of starting an IV infusion of the drug. He was certainly on top of his plan of action.

'I'll draw up an antihistamine and steroids too,' he told Tilly. 'We'll get a twelve lead ECG, chest X-ray, an arterial blood gas and some bloods off to check her urea and electrolyte levels. Could you set up a racemic adrenaline nebuliser, please?' His gaze slid sideways. 'Talia?' He was focused on her face beneath the oxygen mask. 'How's your breathing feeling now? Is it getting any easier?'

But Talia didn't nod. Or shake her head. Her mouth was opening and closing beneath the mask and her eyes were wide and terrified. Then her eyelids fluttered and closed.

'Talia?' Harry was at the end of the bed in a single step. He lowered the end of the bed, pushed the pillows off and tilted her head to open her airway.

'She crashing,' Tilly said quietly. 'Blood pressure and heart rate are dropping.' She turned to pull the airway trolley closer. 'SPO2s under ninety.'

Talia's level of consciousness was also dropping fast and she was clearly struggling to breathe.

'We're losing the airway.' Harry's words were quiet but he was dropping a verbal bombshell.

Charlotte made a distressed sound and stepped back, her fingers pressed to her mouth. This time Harry's gaze caught and held Tilly's for a heartbeat. And then another. The decisions they had to make in this space of time were huge but could mean the difference between life and death for a young woman. A normal intubation via the mouth or even the nose was highly unlikely to be possible due to the swelling of the tissues at the back of the tongue and in the larynx, which left only one alternative to secure an airway in time—to go in through the front of the neck.

There was no time to summon extra help, like the anaesthetist who was currently busy anyway in Resus Two, dealing with the major trauma case. Charlotte was too overwhelmed to be useful, so this was down to Harry and Tilly and part of their swift, silent communication was deciding who was going to perform this invasive procedure. In the end, that decision was as much of a no-brainer as having come to assist Harry in the first place because Tilly thought she saw Harry's confidence falter. Just for a nanosecond, but it was enough.

'I'll do it,' she said.

Oh, *man*...

Tilly couldn't possibly know what was going through Harry's mind in that instant— a flashback to a scene that had started in an almost identical fashion to this and ended in catastrophe—but she saw enough to take the lead and…and it felt like a lifeline. He could—and would—have stepped up to this challenge with every expectation of success but, for this young girl's sake, it was much better for it to be done by someone who didn't have a demon to fight.

He could step back. Not as far as Charlotte had, of course. He could provide the skilled assistance that Tilly needed with drawing up drugs needed and having all the equipment available. He arranged the scalpel, artery forceps, bougie and the endotracheal tube on the sterile drape and made sure he had an ambu bag with an end tidal CO_2 detector attached. He helped position Talia by hyper-extending her neck when the drugs took effect but he didn't have the responsibility of identifying exactly where to make that incision through the cricothyroid membrane and then open it, insert a guidewire and then slide the hollow tube over the top to create a patent airway.

He just needed to hold his breath and hope like hell that Tilly really knew what she was doing.

She certainly seemed to. Her focus was

intense enough to suggest that failure wasn't allowed to be an option, the movements of her hands suggested that this wasn't the first time she'd performed this procedure and within a commendably short space of time the bag mask was attached to the tube and oxygen was flowing to where it needed to go. There was still a lot to do to ensure this patient's condition was stable but, as Tilly's gaze snagged on Harry's as she looked up to check the readings on the monitor, it was an acknowledgment that they were already well on track to a successful outcome in an unexpected crisis. And that they'd done it together, as a team.

He could see something else in her eyes he'd never seen before.

Respect? He knew she'd been impressed at the speed with which he'd managed that tricky IV cannulation but there was an edge of something else in that brush of eye contact and it looked like curiosity. Had she guessed that when a surgical airway had to be done he'd been facing a personal challenge of a scenario he'd never wanted to see repeated? If so, she wasn't judging him for it but rather wondering what it had been about. Maybe he'd tell her about that case at a more appropriate time.

For now, it was enough to know that that ghost had been laid, so he was unlikely to feel that frisson of doubt that could potentially affect his performance if he was ever faced with this situation again.

Which meant that he was most definitely in Dr Matilda Dawson's debt.

Big-time.

CHAPTER TWO

THERE WERE TEARS in those big blue eyes.

'It's okay.' Harry handed Charlotte some tissues. 'It was a pretty confronting situation. You did the right thing by calling for help as fast as you did.'

'I thought she was going to die. And when you had to cut into her throat like that, I thought I was going to faint...'

'Getting her airway secured is what saved her life. And she's doing very well now. She'll need to be kept under observation for a while but she'll be absolutely fine and she knows about her allergy now so she'll be able to wear a medic alert bracelet and it's very unlikely to happen again.'

Charlotte blew her nose. 'I'm not sure I'm cut out for nursing.'

'Give it time,' Harry advised. 'It might just be that Emergency isn't the right fit for you.'

He checked his watch. 'It's time for you to go home now, so have a rest and don't make any big decisions in too much of a hurry.'

Charlotte nodded. 'Thanks ever so much for this talk. I feel a lot better now.'

Harry got to his feet. 'Happy to help.'

'I'd like to say thanks properly.'

'No need.' He opened the door of the office but Charlotte didn't take the hint.

'What are you doing for Christmas?' she asked. 'If you don't have something planned you'd be very welcome at our place for Christmas dinner. My family would love to meet you.'

'Ah… I do have something planned,' Harry lied. 'I'm heading out of town, in fact. With a…a friend.'

'Oh…'

Harry saw the moment that this young nurse gave up any hope of catching his interest. He could almost see her catching hold of a new level of maturity instead.

'I hope you have a wonderful day.' She was smiling now. 'I can't wait. It's my favourite time of the year.'

Harry headed for the staffroom. A cup of coffee before navigating rush-hour traffic to get home might be a good idea. Traffic that would be far worse than usual on one of the last shopping days before Christmas. It certainly wasn't his favourite time of the year. When you didn't have family, the celebration lost any real significance. And when you were somewhere where it was in totally the wrong season it was just...downright unappealing. Frankly, he couldn't wait until it was over.

With the handover of patients complete, the night shift heading home and the day shift getting into gear, the staffroom was almost empty. The only person there was Tilly, who was holding her phone up to her face as she spoke to someone on a video call.

'So there's nothing wrong?' There was still an anxious note in her voice. 'You had me so worried when I saw I'd missed those calls.'

With the room being so quiet, it was easy to hear a male voice. 'No, no, sweetheart. Not at all. I just wanted to know what time to pick you up from the airport tomorrow, that's all.'

Sweetheart? The Ice Queen had someone in her life who called her sweetheart? Harry was almost shaking his head in disbelief as he headed towards the bench, where a glass jug of filter coffee was staying hot on its element. He was about to walk behind Tilly as she told the man what time her flight was due.

'Are you sure Harry can't come too? He'd be more than welcome, you know. He does know how keen I am to meet him, doesn't he?'

Hearing his name was startling enough to make Harry stop in his tracks and turn his head. He could see a much older man on the screen of Tilly's phone. A man who seemed to be staring back at him. Grinning.

'Is this a case of speaking of the devil? Are *you* Harry?'

'I am indeed,' he said. He could feel Tilly flinch. What on earth had she been saying about him to this person?

'This is my father.' Tilly sounded as if she was speaking with her jaw muscles tightly clenched. 'Jim Dawson. Dad...this is Harry Doyle.'

'Delighted to meet you,' the man said. 'And it's about time.'

'Oh?' Harry could feel the tension emanating from Tilly's body. He thought he heard her swear under her breath, in fact, saying a word he wouldn't have expected Dr Dawson to have ever uttered in her life.

Jim hadn't stopped grinning yet. He was looking positively overjoyed. 'Well, you have been going out with my daughter for quite some time now.'

Harry blinked, taking a moment to realise he'd stumbled into something so bizarre he felt like Alice falling down the rabbit hole. Why on earth would Tilly be lying to her father about him being her boyfriend?

Was it possibly because it was making him look this happy?

But why him of all people, when she didn't even *like* him? When sometimes he'd catch a glance that suggested she would prefer it if he didn't actually exist?

He wasn't upset about the deception but, dammit, he was as curious as Alice.

'As I was saying,' Jim continued. 'You'd be more than welcome here for Christmas. Tilly's coming tomorrow so that we've got a bit of time before the big day. We have a lot of fun in these parts. You won't have been to Central Otago before, I'm guessing? Queenstown? Arrowtown?'

'No.' Harry could at least sound genuine

about his response. 'And it's a part of the country I'd love to see.'

It was also out of town. A long way out of town. And hadn't he just told Charlotte that was where he was heading?

No... Spending Christmas with Matilda Dawson? Not going to happen...

'That's settled then.' Jim was looking misty-eyed as he focused on Tilly again. 'I can't tell you how happy I am, sweetheart.'

'Um...' Tilly cleared her throat. 'I've got to go, Dad. I'll call you again later, yeah?'

She ended the call and then got to her feet, turning to glare directly at Harry.

'How *could* you do that?' she demanded, her tone appalled. 'You've just made everything so much *worse*.'

It was the combination that had pushed her over the edge.

Physical fatigue, after a night shift that had included moments of extreme tension, was the base layer, but there were other flavours swirled through the mix. Like that worry about why her father had been so anxious to talk to her and the annoyance that someone like Harry Doyle could get away with doing whatever he wanted in his sex life with total disregard for the damaging effect it could have on other people. On top of that was the real kicker. The sheer, toe-curling, cringe-making embarrassment of having been found out that she was pretending Harry was her boyfriend.

It was a stroke of luck that they were alone in the staffroom but, even if they hadn't been, Tilly might have still lashed out because there was, apparently, quite a fine line between embarrassment and anger. Who knew?

'Whoa...' It seemed that anger might be contagious, judging by Harry's tone. 'I was helping you out there. What did you want me to say? That the likelihood of me being your boyfriend is on a par with the survival of those snowballs in hell?'

'The feeling's mutual, I can assure you,' Tilly snapped.

The expression on Harry's face was one of utter incredulity. 'So *why*?' he demanded. 'Why would you tell your father a lie like that?'

'I *wasn't* lying.' Tilly's statement was vehement. Then she heard her own words and her gaze slid away from his as she cringed inwardly. Anger was rapidly crossing the line to become purely embarrassment. 'It had nothing to do with you,' she muttered. 'I just…borrowed your name because it popped into my head. You'd started work here that day.'

'So you have a boyfriend that has another name?' Harry sounded bewildered now.

'No.' Tilly gritted her teeth. 'I don't *have* a boyfriend. That's the whole point. My father was having a bad day. He'd lost a patient.' Tilly shook her head. Why on earth was she telling Harry any of this? To try and justify being found out telling a huge fib? To try and shift that embarrassment back to what had felt like perfectly justifiable anger? 'Okay… maybe it was a white lie. And I might have used some stuff that was true—like you being Irish and…'

And absolutely gorgeous, with the most amazing blue eyes she'd ever seen…?

She'd certainly said something along those lines but Tilly stomped on that confession before it could emerge.

'And…it doesn't matter what I said. If you want something to be believable, it's got to have at least an element of truth, doesn't it? And I knew how much it would cheer him up to think I'd met someone. He…um… worries about me.'

Those extraordinary blue eyes were resting on her face. Looking unconvinced. He wasn't buying any of this, was he? Tilly felt anxiety start to compete with the embarrassment she was feeling. What if he started thinking that she was indulging in some kind of fantasy about him? What if he shared that thought with someone else? Hospital grapevines loved nothing more than a bit of gossip like that.

Tilly had to make sure that didn't happen. Maybe the only way out of the corner she felt she'd just trapped herself in was to give her explanation more than simply a brush with the truth.

'I worry about him too,' she added quietly. 'He had a bit of a health scare a while back. A transient ischaemic attack that was the first sign he had alarmingly high blood pressure. It's under treatment now and he's fine but…' she couldn't look at Harry as she was revealing the kind of personal information she never told anyone '…but it made me think about what it would have been like if he'd died, you know? If his last thoughts had been to be still worrying about *me*…

That's why I told him what he wanted to hear more than anything else. That I'd met somebody. That I was—*am*—happier than I've ever been.'

The long moment of silence made her finally raise her gaze to find that Harry was still staring at her and, weirdly, for just a heartbeat, it felt as if they were not simply looking at each other but they were *seeing* each other for the first time ever. But he looked away the instant her gaze touched his and that feeling of connection was broken.

'I'm sorry if I've made things difficult for you.' His voice was slightly distant, as if he was actually thinking about something else. 'But I *was* trying to help. I owed you a favour and I thought that going along with your game might be a way to repay you.'

Curiosity was enough to distract Tilly from trying to decide if she'd rescued herself. 'Repay me for what?'

'It's kind of a long story.'

'I'm listening.' Her tone could probably have been interpreted as a demand for an explanation but this was a great way of shifting attention away from herself. It was definitely the way to stop thinking about that odd moment of connection and possibly a means to end this awkward conversation altogether.

Harry shrugged. 'Short version, then. The last time I had a patient who needed a surgical airway was for a child with a traumatic facial injury. It was about ten years ago on one of my first shifts ever in an ED. I was in a small rural hospital on a night shift with only another junior doctor who thought he knew what he was doing, but he didn't. He walked out when he knew he'd stuffed up and I had to try and carry on but…it was too late.'

Tilly swallowed. She could imagine the carnage. The horror. The heartbreak. She could feel an unexpected and distinct empathy with a newly qualified Harry.

'I've done controlled cricothyroidotomies since then but it was something I never wanted to have to face again in an emergency situation.'

He caught Tilly's gaze again as he spoke and she found she couldn't look away. For once, there was no flirtatious gleam in that grey-blue of a moody sea. She was more aware of what she could feel than see in them, anyway. And it was something totally honest.

'I've lost that fear now,' he added quietly. 'Thanks to being a part of the way you handled that situation.'

'You would have handled it just as well as I did,' Tilly said. She meant it too. She'd seen the way he worked. She'd recognised an impressive level of skill.

His single nod wasn't arrogant in any way. It was an acknowledgement of a fact. 'But, if there's ever a next time, I'll remember tonight and it will make a difference.'

Tilly caught her bottom lip between her teeth. The thought that Harry might be thinking about her at some point in the future was providing another frisson of an unexpected connection. Purely a professional one, of course, which was far more acceptable.

'So that's why I didn't tell your father I had no idea what you were talking about,' Harry said. 'It was my way of saying thanks. And, to be fair, I was being just as dishonest as you were. I'm guessing that you had a reason for lying.'

Tilly let her breath out in a sigh. 'Haven't you ever told a white lie? To try and make someone feel better?'

Harry made a sound like a huff of laughter. 'About two minutes ago,' he admitted. 'I said I was going out of town for Christmas. I needed an excuse for not accepting an invitation but I didn't want to hurt her feelings.'

Tilly's breath escaped in an unamused huff. 'So Charlotte hasn't given up, then?'

The expression on Harry's face made Tilly think she might have to reconsider her opinion that he toyed with the women who threw themselves at him with no regard for their feelings. She also remembered Charlotte telling her that she'd known the interest she felt was not reciprocated. Perhaps Harry's mistake had been being so careful not to hurt her feelings in the first place?

His rueful expression was fading. 'Hey… I *could* be out of town for Christmas, which would mean it wasn't any kind of a lie. Your dad just invited me. And he lives in Queenstown? That's, like, way up there on any tourist's list of "must see" places in New Zealand.'

'Don't be ridiculous.' Tilly's tone was sharper than merited but she was trying— and failing—to ignore that smile. 'You're not coming home with me.'

'But I've got a few days off. And it would make your dad so happy.' Harry's tone was teasing. 'Did you see the way he couldn't stop smiling? I think he approves of your choice already.'

Tilly was shaking her head as she turned to reach for her shoulder bag, hooked over the back of a chair, but she couldn't stop her brain conjuring up a fleeting image. Of her. With Harry beside her and her father confidently waiting for the signs of a deep, romantic connection between them. Signs that she would have as much chance of producing as those snowballs Harry had mentioned. She couldn't stop the frisson of something unpleasant skating over her skin either. An echo from the past?

'There's a word for women like you... Frigid, that's what...like something straight from the freezer that nobody wants to touch...'

Tilly also knew what her nickname was around here. She could assume that Harry had also heard it so that just made his suggestion of keeping up the deception in real life even more ridiculous.

But, yeah…she *had* seen how happy her father had looked when he thought he was meeting the man she'd been seeing for a couple of months now. She hadn't seen him look that happy since…well, she couldn't remember when.

And the desire to make him happy had been there for as long as Tilly could remember. The pride and love in that smile touched a part of her heart that was so tender it always made tears only a blink away.

But she shook her head again, more decisively this time.

'As you pointed out so charmingly,' she said, her back still to Harry, 'a snowball would have to stay frozen in hell for us to be in a relationship. My father is a very intelligent man. He'd see through you in a heartbeat.'

'Are you sure?' Harry sounded curious. 'Because I missed my vocation really. I could have been an actor.'

Tilly heard raw emotion in the growling sound Harry suddenly made and then froze as she felt his hands on her shoulders. She could feel his breath on the back of her neck.

'It was love at first sight,' Harry murmured, his Irish accent more pronounced than ever. 'And now…well… I just can't imagine the rest of my life without you in it, Tilly…'

Dear Lord… She might be frozen to the

spot but there was a heat surrounding her that felt as if it could melt her bones. A heat like nothing she'd ever felt. A heat that she would never have believed she was even capable of feeling because, well…because frigid women couldn't feel that kind of heat, could they? But she *had* felt it and it must have been enough to fry her brain cells because, while Harry had been uttering them, she had believed every word. And she desperately wanted to hang on to that feeling, but Harry lifted his hands and the spell was broken instantly.

'See what I did there?'

Tilly was taking her time to turn and face Harry directly as she let any effects he'd had on her evaporate, but she could hear the grin in his voice.

'That could get nominated for an Oscar, so it could.' There was satisfaction in Harry's tone. 'Don't you think? How happy would that make your dad? It might be his best Christmas ever.'

'But it would be a lie.'

'A white lie,' Harry corrected her. 'Like the one I told. And maybe *two* white lies will cancel each other out and neither of us would need to feel guilty about anything.' He lifted his eyebrows. 'It's a win-win situation. I get to escape town and get to see a place every visitor should see. You get to make your father a happy, happy man. If you tell him down the track that things didn't work out and I've gone back to Ireland, well... that's nobody's fault, is it? It's just life...'

'You can*not* be serious.' Tilly was incredulous. 'You're actually offering to come home with me for Christmas and pretend to be my boyfriend?'

The smile on Harry's face evaporated in the sudden silence that fell between them. A silence that was stretching into something significant. Tilly could see the muscles in his throat contract as he swallowed and, when he spoke, his voice sounded a little raw, even.

'We've got more in common than you might think,' he said quietly. 'I wish it had occurred to me to try and give my mother the hope that everything she might have wished for me to have in life was just around the corner but... I never got the chance.' He gave his head a small shake. 'I get that this thing with your father is nothing to do with me, but I've kind of got involved now and...'

His voice trailed off but Tilly could imagine the words that weren't being uttered. And if he helped her, could it perhaps go some way towards making up for not having been able to do it for his own mother?

She was lost for words herself, with this glimpse of an emotional depth she would never have associated with this man, but the suspicion that he might be simply giving her another demonstration of his acting skills emerged as he smiled at her again.

'We could make it work,' he said. 'It might even be kind of fun. What do you say?'

Harry's smile stretched into a grin that could only be described as cheeky. It made Tilly imagine what this man had been like as a kid. His mother must have loved him to bits. A happy, mischievous little boy who probably got away with almost anything because he'd been born with the ability to charm those around him and make the world feel like a better place.

Her father deserved to feel like that. Especially at Christmastime.

A tiny shiver ran down Tilly's spine as she thought of that heat Harry had conjured up from nowhere with just the touch of his hands and the tone of his voice. It hadn't been real—he'd only been acting—but, just for a heartbeat, it had made Tilly remember a time when she'd believed that dreams could come true.

That the world was indeed a much better place than it had turned out to be.

And…maybe it would be nice to feel like that again. Even if it was just a pretence. Even if it was only for Christmas.

'I'll think about it,' she said.

CHAPTER THREE

'So…WHAT MADE you say yes in the end?'

'I rang my dad back after I'd caught up on some sleep. He'd had a really busy day and looked beyond tired, but he was so excited about my visit and meeting you and…' Tilly leaned her head back, shifting her gaze to look out of the small, oval aircraft window.

And she couldn't possibly tell Harry about how it had made her feel as her father had talked about him being there with her. How appealing the idea of spending more time in his company had become. The internal tussle that the memory of the heat his touch had created had kept her awake long after that phone call because, deep down, Tilly realised it might actually be possible to pull off that deception for a couple of days and there might be a reason she wanted to do it that had nothing to do with making her father happy.

A purely selfish reason. Because she couldn't deny that part of her wanted to know if it was possible to feel that heat again.

Did she want to feel it?

Yes, of course she did. It was clearly something as desirable as finding shelter when you'd been out in the cold for far too long.

But no. She didn't want to feel it because it was terrifying. It couldn't be trusted. It could lead to getting very, very badly burnt. Even if it was only a pretence, Tilly was, quite literally, playing with fire.

Not that Harry had the slightest clue what was flashing through her mind in that instant, and that had been the real reason that Tilly had ended up saying yes. Because she knew she could control how she felt enough for no one else to guess the truth. Even her father.

Or, thank goodness, Harry.

Keeping her feelings hidden was a skill she'd perfected over many years. She could turn on the 'Ice Queen' persona with no more than a mental flick of a switch.

She could feel Harry's gaze on the back of her head. He was still waiting for her to finish explaining what had led to him sitting in the seat beside her, wasn't he?

'And…' Tilly let her breath out as she found something plausible to say. 'I couldn't bring myself to tell him you couldn't come after all and disappoint him again.'

'Again?' Harry sounded astonished. 'I would have thought having a daughter like you would be something he's very proud of.'

Oh… Tilly let herself absorb what sounded like a compliment. An unexpected one, given that they hadn't yet started their role play for her father's benefit.

'My dad's dream was that I would become a doctor and then take over his family practice.'

'And it's not your dream?'

'It was when I was a kid. Before I knew any better.' She threw Harry a wry smile. 'Along with the dream of getting married and raising half a dozen kids in the old family homestead.'

'Not going to happen, then?' Harry suggested.

'Not in this lifetime. But I suspect Dad's been waiting every year for the announcement that I'm coming home for good for at least the last five or six years. That's probably more than enough disappointment, wouldn't you say?'

'So…where is it you used to live? I've forgotten.'

'The practice is in Craig's Gully, which is about halfway between Arrowtown and Cutler's Creek. Family homestead's out of town a bit on a remnant of the original sheep station.'

'And that's not somewhere you'd want to live again?'

Tilly stopped herself rolling her eyes. 'Did you grow up in a small country town? The kind where absolutely everybody knows absolutely everybody else's business?'

'I grew up in Dublin. Big city.' Harry lifted an eyebrow. 'You should probably know that about your Irish boyfriend.'

Tilly stifled a sigh. He was right. How on earth had she convinced herself that this was a good idea? She might be an expert in hiding her feelings but she had to admit she was beginning to feel very uncharacteristically nervous. She hadn't really thought this through properly, had she?

She cleared her throat. 'So…do you still have family there? Your dad? Any siblings?'

'No.'

There was something in that single quiet word that made Tilly catch her breath as she remembered that glimpse of a part of Harry she hadn't realised existed. Someone who had had a mother he'd cared enough about to have wished he could make her happy before she died. She would have caught Harry's gaze as well, but he was looking down at his hands.

'That's why I left Ireland, to be fair. There was nothing left to keep me there.'

Something in Harry's tone suggested that he wouldn't be keen on answering any more personal questions and that was fine by Tilly. If they both had things they'd rather keep private it would be easier to keep a safe distance.

Harry leaned in front of Tilly, so that he could see out of the window properly, and he let his breath out in a silent whistle seconds later.

'There's nothing but mountains down there. You wouldn't want to be having a crash landing, would you?'

Tilly laughed. 'Is now the time to tell you that Queenstown is one of more challenging airports in the world to land at because of all the surrounding mountains?'

As if to back up her statement, the plane tilted as it began a turn. There would be a few more of them before they landed but Tilly was used to the complicated approach. She hoped they would be coming in over the lake and then looping to land in the opposite direction, which gave the best view of Queenstown and this stunning part of the country. She might have no intention of coming back here to live but this was her home. Part of her DNA.

Weirdly, she was starting to feel excited by the idea of showing it off to Harry. It shouldn't matter at all but she wanted him to love it as much as she did.

Harry Doyle had done a few impulsive things in his time.

Okay, more than a few, but it only dawned on him as he heard Tilly laugh that he might have bitten off a bit more than he could comfortably chew this time—when it was far too late to even think of changing his mind.

Despite the engine noise, the sound of Tilly's laughter was hanging in the air between them and, from what Harry could see through the window, it seemed as if they might be on track to fly straight into a mountain that looked disconcertingly close to the aircraft. Thank goodness the pilot was starting another turn but there were some patchy lumps of cloud that were dense enough to cut visibility to nothing as they continued their descent and Harry could feel a knot of tension forming in his gut.

Maybe it was better not to watch. He sat back in his seat and closed his eyes for a moment. It wasn't as if worrying about the safety of this flight path was going to change anything.

It would also be a complete waste of time to wonder if he should have backed out of this impulsive offer to go home with Tilly for Christmas when he'd had the chance. Because he'd never really had that chance in the first place, had he?

Not when Tilly had told him why she'd lied to her father. When he'd known exactly how she must have felt when she'd got that call to tell her that he was potentially very ill. Maybe she'd got the news before they'd been able to diagnose a TIA and she might have thought he was being rushed to hospital with a stroke that could have been fatal. Listening to her had been a bit of a shock, in fact, because it had taken him straight back to when he'd got the news about his mother and how terrible that journey had been to try and get back to her in time.

How devastating it had been to fail.

He'd also caught a glimpse of a completely different person beneath that cool, reserved exterior that was the only side he'd ever seen of Dr Matilda Dawson. Someone who could get angry—passionate, even—when she was trying to protect a person she cared about. Someone who had lied to her father about having a significant relationship in her life because she knew it would make him happy. Was it simply that her father would want to know her future was secure or had Jim Dawson been worried that his daughter was lonely in her current life?

Was she lonely?

Not that that was any of his business either, but the idea that Tilly was vulnerable beneath that icy shell would have made it difficult to back out. That slightly shocking sense of connection he'd felt listening to her fear that she might have caused her father any worry on his deathbed had made it completely impossible.

And Harry hadn't been kidding when he told her he was an expert actor. How could he not be when he'd honed that skill as a child, learning not only how to make friends and entertain his peers by being the class clown with every new school he attended but to hide his own emotions to avoid being bullied and…yeah…to hide the fear, even from himself, that came from being lonely.

It might have been in his imagination but it felt as if the connection that had come from nowhere was on both sides. A very different kind of connection to the one they'd created earlier yesterday by dealing with a professional crisis together.

And it had been fun to give her that demonstration of his talents, hadn't it?

He hadn't really expected Tilly to say yes when she'd phoned him last night, but he hadn't had the time or inclination to unpick the reason why there seemed to be a solid barrier to backing away from that offer. Besides, it was only for a day or two and… well…it was Christmas, wasn't it? A time of peace and kindness to all.

But Harry had never heard Tilly laugh before and he found he was hanging onto the echo of that sound. Because he liked it.

He liked it a lot.

The touch on his arm made his eyes fly open again.

'Look…' Tilly was still smiling. 'You're missing something special.'

She wasn't wrong. The view from the window was spectacular. Below the clouds now, the plane was banking steeply. He could see a wall of mountains. A river. Sheep that seemed close enough to count and barren hilltops that felt near enough for the wingtips to brush. Harry could see the vast blue stretch of water that was still enough to be reflecting the surrounding peaks as they sank towards a runway at the end of the lake.

Harry was soaking it in, his head close to Tilly's as they shared the window. He didn't turn his head but he could sense that she was still smiling. And he thought he could hear another soft echo of her laughter.

That was something unexpectedly special too, wasn't it?

'He's not here.' Tilly's gaze raked over Queenstown Airport's small arrivals area.

'We might be a bit earlier than expected. He's not to know that we only had carry-on luggage.'

'More likely that he's been caught up in

some kind of emergency. We might be waiting for a while.'

An announcement came through the loudspeaker system as she finished speaking.

'Dr Matilda Dawson, please report to the main information desk.'

Tilly threw an 'I told you so' glance at Harry. 'Come on. We'd better go and find out what's going on.'

The message waiting at the desk was that Dr Jim Dawson was in the emergency department of Queenstown Hospital.

'Did he say how long he might be?' Tilly queried.

'No, sorry. But the message came through a couple of hours ago, so maybe it won't be too much longer?'

'Let me buy you lunch while we're waiting,' Harry suggested. 'It looked like quite a nice café we just walked past.'

'The hospital's very close to the airport. Let's wander over and see what's happening. A couple of hours is a long time to be waiting to transfer a patient.' Now that she was standing on home ground, waiting to start the grand deception, that nervousness was becoming more pronounced and her father's absence was only making it worse. What else might be lying in wait to provide unexpected challenges that could instantly expose the deception?

The heat of the midday sun hit them as they walked out of the air-conditioned airport and Tilly wished she hadn't worn her jeans.

'I might take you down to the river this afternoon,' she told Harry. 'We'll need a swim if it stays this warm. Did you bring your togs?'

'My *what*?'

'Togs.' Tilly turned her head to catch Harry's expression. Did he not understand New Zealand slang? 'A bathing costume? Swim-shorts? Budgie smugglers?'

Harry made a slightly strangled sound and Tilly realised that she might have misinterpreted his expression. Maybe it was the idea of being semi-clothed with someone who was pretty much a total stranger that had startled him. Her throwaway suggestion had suddenly become a big deal.

A big, awkward deal that was definitely a new challenge. This was way worse than not knowing that the man who was supposed to be her boyfriend had grown up in Dublin.

This was about not even being comfortable in each other's company.

Except that she'd forgotten about Harry's acting skills. And perhaps he'd seen a flash of something like panic in her face that the plan was going to fall over before it could even begin. Because he was grinning now. He was back in control.

'Didn't think of bringing my togs,' he said lightly. 'I might have to go skinny-dipping.'

Oh, *help*…

Any relief that she'd only need to follow Harry's lead in this pretence to make it work faded as Tilly felt her cheeks heating up faster than could be attributed purely to the strength of the direct sunshine they were walking in. If the thought of Harry Doyle swimming naked could make her this flustered, could even Harry's acting skills convince her father that they were more than simply colleagues? He'd see straight through this farce the moment he clapped eyes on them, wouldn't he?

Or maybe he wouldn't. Tilly found her father in a very unexpected place within the emergency department of the district hospital. And in a very unexpected condition. One that made it unlikely that he would notice anything odd about his daughter's relationship with her boyfriend.

'I'm as high as a kite, love,' he told his daughter. 'Needed a bit of jungle juice while they got my bones back into the right place.' He beamed at Harry. 'Gidday, mate. Sorry I wasn't at the airport to meet you.'

'Not a problem, Dr Dawson.' Harry eyed the heavy-duty moon boot on the older man's lower leg and foot. 'Looks like you've been in the wars.'

'Call me Jim, son. You're practically part of the family.'

'Dad…' Tilly's tone was a warning. 'Don't go starting any rumours. Or scaring Harry off.'

But, again, Harry was laughing. He draped his arm around Tilly's shoulders. 'I don't scare that easily,' he told Jim. 'Or I wouldn't be here at all, would I?'

Jim was nodding sagely. 'We'd better do what we're told. Tilly's the boss.'

Both men laughed as if sharing a private joke and Tilly found herself scowling as she shrugged off the weight of Harry's arm. 'What happened, exactly?' she demanded.

'Your dad fell off a ladder.' The nurse who came into the room made a tutting sound.

'He should know better at his age, but there you go...'

'You're making me sound decrepit, Liz,' Jim complained. 'I'm not that old.'

'You're over seventy,' Tilly reminded her father. 'What on earth were you doing up a ladder, anyway?'

'Putting up the Christmas lights. And those Santa legs that stick out of the chimney. The ones that made you laugh so much when you were a little girl?'

Tilly shook her head. 'I'm not five years old now, Dad. What's the damage?'

'Fracture dislocation of the ankle,' the nurse said. 'He wanted to avoid surgery. The fracture's not displaced and the dislocation seems to have been successfully reduced, but it'll need careful monitoring for the next few days. We were going to admit him to keep him out of trouble.'

'No need.' Jim Dawson was shaking his head firmly. 'Why would I need to stay in hospital when I've got two doctors to look after me in my own home?'

Liz gave Tilly a long-suffering glance. 'Would you believe he drove himself in here?'

Tilly closed her eyes. 'I would.'

'The truck's automatic,' Jim Dawson said. 'It was only my left foot that wasn't working.'

'His car's still parked in the ambulance bay,' Liz said. 'But there is a bed here if you think it's in his best interests to stay.'

It might be in her own best interests to have her father safely tucked up in a hospital bed for the next day or two because it would make this game with Harry so much easier, but it was already very clear that Jim Dawson was not about to give in without a fight. He was already starting to climb off the bed.

'There's no way I'm going to miss having a proper Christmas with my daughter,' he announced. 'Life's too short not to make the most of this kind of precious time together.'

Tilly closed her eyes for a heartbeat. The reminder that life could, indeed, be shorter than expected was precisely why she'd started this in the first place.

'And this is her boyfriend, Liz.' Jim's tone was a mix of pride and delight. 'He's an Irish lad.'

'So I noticed.'

Tilly opened her eyes in time to see Harry smile at the middle-aged nurse, who smiled back without hesitation. She stifled a sigh.

Dr Harry Doyle could charm the birds out of the trees if he wanted to, couldn't he? But there was a silver lining in the cloud of her father's unfortunate accident in that it would provide a distraction that could excuse anything that might not fit with the glow of the happy couple she and Harry were supposed to be. Her nervousness was starting to evaporate now that introductions had been taken care of and Harry seemed perfectly at ease.

'Stay there for a tick, Jim.' Harry stepped forward, his arm out to prevent an attempt to stand unaided. 'You don't want to be putting any weight on that foot.' He turned to his new friend. 'Lizzie, would you possibly have a wheelchair we could borrow?'

It wasn't only a collapsible wheelchair that was made available to one of the district's longest serving general practitioners. Everybody wanted to contribute. Pillows were provided to cushion the leg on the raised footrest. Elbow crutches appeared and medications, including some potent painkillers, were dispensed, along with a warning from the consultant.

'I'm well aware you're qualified enough to be teaching me a thing or two, Tilly,' he said, 'but I remember patching you up more than once when you fell off your pony and that doesn't seem that long ago. Plus, I wouldn't be doing my job if I didn't tell you to bring him straight back in if you notice any changes, like increased pain or swelling.'

Tilly nodded. 'Compartment syndrome will be at the top of my list for possible complications. Don't worry, I'll be keeping a very close watch.'

'And don't let him put any weight whatsoever on that foot until we've seen him again.'

'I'll do my best.' Tilly gave her father a stern glance. 'Did you hear that, Dad? If you don't behave you'll be back in here like a shot.'

Harry was holding the handles on the back of the wheelchair. He leaned down to speak in a stage whisper. 'Tilly's the boss, remember? We both have to do what we're told.'

'I've made an outpatient appointment for Boxing Day for you, Jim.' The consultant lifted an eyebrow. 'That's only three days away. You can behave that long, can't you?'

Tilly looked at the way her father was smiling as he nodded. She had her doubts about just how well he was going to behave. Then she lifted her gaze to catch Harry's and… yeah…she had her doubts about *him* too.

But that *smile*…

It was doing odd things to her. Like making her very thankful he was here, now that her nervousness was almost gone. Like making her feel he was on her side and that she wasn't dealing with this unexpected personal event alone. A feeling that was enough to create a very strange melting sensation somewhere deep in her gut that took a firm mental shove to dismiss.

Harry's being here was only because he'd agreed to take part in a performance that was intended to give her father a Christmas to remember. And, although it felt as if the wheels were already falling off any plans she might have had for the next couple of days, it was far too late to back out of this by telling her father the truth. She only had to think about that look on his face when he'd told Harry he was practically part of the family and the proud note in his voice when he'd told Liz that Harry was her boyfriend to know how much it would hurt him to find out it wasn't true. The physical pain he was in at the moment was quite enough to be a shadow on any Christmas celebrations without her throwing another major blow on top of it.

Tilly knew what she had to do. For the sake of everybody involved in this pretence. 'Let's get this show on the road,' she said.

CHAPTER FOUR

THE OLD, SLIGHTLY BATTERED double-cab utility vehicle felt like a small bus to Harry as he sat in the front passenger seat, but Tilly was handling it as if it was no more difficult to drive than a small hatchback car. She was driving fast but competently, taking the curves of the road carefully to minimise any discomfort to her father, who was propped up sideways on the back seat to keep his broken ankle elevated.

Harry would have been impressed with this unexpected splinter skill Tilly was demonstrating but, to be honest, there was too much else competing for that head space. He wasn't even paying much attention to the conversation about local people and events that Tilly was having with her father until he dozed off. He was feeling very happy that he'd decided to come on this rather unusual break from the city. No wonder this area of the country was one of the top tourist destinations in the world. It felt as if Tilly was the one doing him a favour now, not the other way around.

The countryside they were driving through was extraordinary. It wasn't just the towering mountains all around them, there were stretches of sparkling blue water in more than one lake and a huge, fast-flowing river between dramatic cliffs when the road cut through a gorge. The barren dryness of rock-studded hills with clumps of golden tussock but not a blade of green grass to be seen was more than balanced by vineyards that stretched as far as the eye could see with lush foliage.

They went through a small township with stone-built cottages, a picturesque church and an outdoor produce market that could have been a summer destination in Europe, past another small lake and more vineyards before turning into a long, tree-lined driveway that led up the slope of a hill.

'Home sweet home,' Tilly announced as the house came into view.

It was another surprise for Harry, this graceful old wooden house with a slate roof that sat tucked into the hill with wide verandas, bay windows and an elegant turret on one corner. It was hugged by terraced gardens and trees, lawns and small paddocks. Tilly slowed the vehicle as they drove past a shaggy pony with its head over a gate.

'That's Spud,' she told Harry. 'He's the same age as me.'

'No way,' Harry said. He couldn't resist teasing her a little. 'Surely ponies don't live that long, do they?'

'Some get past forty years old.' Tilly's glance suggested she couldn't decide whether or not he was joking. 'But thirty-four *is* getting on a bit for a pony.'

She peered up at the roof of the house as she stopped the car. Harry followed her gaze to see the inflatable red legs with black boots visible above an old clay chimney pot.

'I'm definitely too old to find Santa legs in the chimney the funniest thing ever.' Tilly sounded exasperated. 'I can't believe you thought that was a good idea, Dad.'

'It's been a while since you were home, sweetheart,' Jim Dawson said quietly. 'I wanted it to be special.'

Tilly's gaze caught Harry's, just for a heartbeat, as she turned towards the back seat. He was already sensing undercurrents of things that weren't being said and he couldn't miss the flash of something in Tilly's eyes that made it suddenly difficult to catch his breath.

Sadness?

No…it was more like a brush of helplessness. Something deeper than vulnerability, even. An admission of failure to fix something because it was simply impossible?

'It *is* special, Dad.'

Her tone had a note in it that Harry had never heard before and he could feel a pull towards something else that was as unexpected as everything else he was discovering since he'd got himself entangled with Matilda Dawson's personal life. A bit disturbing, in fact. It was almost as if he was getting a glimpse of the shattered remains of the dream that both Tilly and her father had once shared of her future.

Jim might have told him he was practically a part of the family, but that was the last thing Harry wanted to be. He was here as a favour to Tilly. If pretending to be her boyfriend was going to be as much fun as he'd hoped—for everybody involved—he needed to take control of these twists and turns as competently as Tilly had done when she'd been driving that vehicle through the gorge. He needed to lighten up.

He opened the door of the ute. 'I'll get the wheelchair out of the back.'

The walk-in pantry attached to the large kitchen in Tilly's childhood home had been stocked with enough food to feed a small army for any Christmas celebrations.

She made ham sandwiches for their lunch, with thick slices of juicy ham on the bone, wholegrain mustard and tomatoes and crisp lettuce fresh from the garden between soft wedges of sourdough bread. They could have eaten at the comfortable everyday table in the kitchen or the formal mahogany table that could seat twelve people in the dining room, but she ended up serving the meal like a picnic on a coffee table in the living room.

Her father was now ensconced on the huge old sofa with its comfortable feather-stuffed cushions that was positioned in front of a wide bay window offering a view that stretched across vineyards to the craggy rocks of what had always felt like a private mountain range to Tilly. He had pillows behind his back and under his leg but, instead of resting, he was leaning sideways, opening the flaps of a cardboard box that she could see was full of Christmas decorations. There were more boxes stacked up at the end of the couch that Harry must have ferried in while she'd been preparing lunch and he came in with a very long box that Tilly knew contained an ancient artificial Christmas tree as she set the tray down on the coffee table.

'I did tell Jim he needed to be resting,' he said. 'We can do the tree later.' He eyed the sandwiches on the tray. 'Those look good.'

'Christmas ham,' Tilly told him. 'You'll be sick of it by halfway through January, but you can't beat the first taste of it.'

'Glazed gammon's a taste of home.' Harry nodded as he took a plate and helped himself to a sandwich. 'It was a favourite of my mam's.'

'What else is traditional for Christmas dinner in Ireland?' Jim asked. 'I got everything I could think of yesterday, so you'd feel right at home. There's a turkey, of course, and I'm sure Tilly can look up a recipe for bread sauce. And there's Brussels sprouts and we can pick fresh peas from my garden. And potatoes. You'll be able to fill your boots with potatoes. I've even got duck fat to roast them in.'

Harry laughed. 'You're lucky you Kiwis get associated with a bird. The first thing anyone thinks of when they hear an Irish accent is a potato, which is far less interesting.' He shook his head. 'Don't get me wrong, though. I love potatoes. And I guess it's an Irish tradition to have more than one sort on the table at Christmas. Roast potatoes, mashed potatoes and my favourite— when they're sliced and baked with cheese and onions and they go all brown and crispy on top.'

'Potato gratin,' Tilly said. 'Not something I've ever had with Christmas dinner.'

'There's a first time for everything,' Jim said.

'Don't go to any trouble on my account.' Harry's wave was dismissing his favourite potato dish. 'It does seem strange that you eat a hot dinner in the middle of a summer's day, but turkey and roast potatoes sounds like the perfect Christmas dinner to me.'

'Hopefully I'll feel hungry by then.' Jim shook his head as Tilly offered him a plate. 'I'll just have a cup of tea, thanks, love.'

Tilly looked at the lines of pain she could

see on her father's face. 'I'll get you a dose of your painkillers too. Maybe you can sleep for a bit this afternoon.'

But Jim shook his head. 'I can't do that. What if I'm needed?'

'Surely you're not on call? The clinic's closed for the next few days, isn't it?'

'Yes…but you know I'm always on call. Some of my patients have been coming to me for their whole lives and they know I'm always on call for them. And I've got Maggie Grimshaw, who's home from the hospice to have a last Christmas with her family on the farm. She's got a syringe driver for her pain meds that I need to refill every day. And I promised I'd be available to help in any way I can.'

'Oh, no…' Tilly could see that Harry had abandoned his sandwich as he listened to their conversation. 'Dad went to school with Maggie,' she told him. 'They've known each other their entire lives. She's been battling cancer for a long time but…' She let her breath out in a sigh. 'It makes it so much harder, doesn't it, dealing with something like this at Christmastime.' She turned back to Jim. 'I'd be more than happy to cover that for you, Dad. Maggie was like another mum to me.' Tilly swallowed hard. 'The only one, sometimes, when Mum was away so often.'

'I could help too,' Harry said, his tone sombre. 'With any calls that you want to respond to. I've worked as a general practitioner in rural areas, Jim. In Canada and England. I've also done stints in developing countries, so I've had enough experience to be ready to tackle anything.' He was smiling now. 'And Tilly and I work very well together. We make the best team.'

Tilly found herself smiling as well, a warm glow curling through her body at the praise of how good a team they made. It was true. It might have only been the first time they'd worked together in dealing with that anaphylactic shock but it had been seamless. Smooth. As if they had worked together for a very long time.

Jim's smile was suspiciously misty as he looked from Harry to Tilly and then back again. 'You couldn't have said anything to make me happier, son,' he said quietly. 'I'll have a word with Maggie soon and let her know what's going on.'

'We could drop in this afternoon, perhaps,' Tilly said briskly, shutting down that glow before the warmth became an uncomfortable heat. 'When I take Harry for a bit of a tiki tour.'

'A tiki tour?'

'It means having a good look around.' Tilly handed her father the cup of tea she'd poured. 'Harry's still learning Kiwi,' she told him. 'He didn't know what togs were either.'

'I am learning a lot,' Harry agreed. He waved his hand towards a section of wall beside where the Christmas tree was standing, that was covered in framed photographs. 'Why didn't you tell me that your mother was an international model? Or that you're half Italian?'

Jim didn't seem to notice the brief awkward silence between them. 'Chiara pretty much gave up the modelling not long after she married me,' he said. 'Her merino wool fashion business took off and she wanted to spend more time with her horses. Oh…that reminds me. I'm supposed to be judging the dress-ups at the pony club Christmas do later today. I can't let them down.'

'I'm sure they won't mind if I step in to help with that,' Tilly assured him. 'It was only because of me that you got involved with the pony club in the first place, after all.'

'But what about tomorrow?' Jim was

frowning deeply. 'I'm always Father Christmas at the village barbecue. I've done that for fifty years. I'm not about to let someone else do it.'

'You might have to,' Tilly warned.

'There's nobody that could do it like I do,' Jim muttered. 'And the kids think I'm the real thing. They'll stop believing there's a Santa Claus.'

'It might be a bit of a giveaway that Santa's wearing the same big boot on his foot and using crutches just like their family doctor.' Tilly picked up her sandwich. 'They're not going to guess it's not you if someone's wearing the full outfit with that padded stomach and the bushy fake beard.'

'It's not just what I look like. It's how I talk to the kiddies. And what I say.'

'You've got time to pass on all your Santa wisdom,' Tilly told him. 'So all you really need is a good actor to take on the role. It's a good thing I happened to bring one with me, isn't it?'

From nowhere, Tilly could suddenly hear an echo of Harry's voice.

'I missed my vocation, really. I could have been an actor...'

And it wasn't only his voice that she was

remembering. She could almost feel the touch of his hands on her shoulders and that heat that had been generated in her entire body. The heat that she'd both wanted, but been so scared, to feel again was hovering just out of reach, like a fragment of a dream that was playing hard to catch.

Tilly took a big bite of her sandwich. Because she didn't dare catch Harry's gaze. He might guess the turmoil that was going on as the reactions of her body and brain vied for emotional supremacy. That a part of her wanted nothing more than for him to touch her again.

But an even bigger part wanted nothing more than to run as fast and as far away from him as possible.

No… Harry couldn't believe what he was hearing. A dress-up competition? A village party? Dressing up in a full Father Christmas outfit with its long sleeves and fur trim and probably an itchy fake beard and moustache and then cooking in blazing summer sunshine?

It was more than weird.

It was…

Perfect, that was what it was. Utterly foreign, which meant there was no danger of it reminding him of any Christmas from his childhood or stirring up the sadness of losing his only family, which had been the main reason he'd left his home country in the first place.

In fact, the more he threw himself into whatever bizarre traditions that were followed in this part of the world, the easier this was going to be. It really would be acting, and he hadn't been lying when he'd told Tilly he was good at it. He was so good at it, in fact, that it was automatic. Often, he didn't even need to make a conscious effort.

Like now, as he let his smile widen until he looked like he was being offered an opportunity he'd always wanted.

'Sounds like this is going to be a Christmas to remember,' he said. 'Bring it on.'

'They don't really dress up the ponies, do they?'

'Of course. I won the first prize when I was eight. Spud had a unicorn horn on his bridle, a pink mane and tail and glitter all over and I had the most beautiful princess dress and a cone hat with a long veil.'

Tilly was driving her own vehicle—a

rugged old Jeep that had as many scrapes and dents as her father's ute—as she took Harry for his 'tiki tour' that would eventually see them attend the finale of the local pony club's Christmas event.

Currently, they were on an unsealed private road that was part of the Grimshaws' high country sheep station, winding through hills that were providing an increasingly impressive view. The drop off the side of the road was slightly hair-raising at times, however. Like when they came around a tight down sloping bend to find a small mob of sheep in the middle of the road. Tilly braked instantly and then turned the vehicle into the direction of a skid that could have sent them sideways into a fence, with all the skill of a rally driver, before bringing the Jeep to a halt. It was seriously impressive.

'Where on earth did you learn to drive like this?'

'Right here.' Tilly's gesture took in the countryside stretched out below them before being cut off by distant mountains. 'Dad taught me to drive by making me his chauffeur on all his weekend call-outs. Shingle roads, four-wheel driving off road, unexpected encounters with livestock, black ice and dealing with snowstorms was all part of the training.' She threw Harry a wry smile as she drove slowly towards the sheep, who were now standing completely still, staring at the vehicle. 'It was a different story trying to deal with rush hour traffic in a big city, mind you. I hated it for a long time.' She tooted the horn and the sheep finally began moving out of their way.

'Do we need to get them off the road and back into the field?'

Tilly shook her head. 'They're grazing the long acre.'

Harry snorted. 'You really do talk a different language around here.'

'It's the grass verge on either side of the road. Easier to let the sheep out to eat it down than use a tractor to mow it. You'll see farmers using electric fences on public roads, but this is private land. There'll be another gate you can open soon, and we'll make sure it's shut behind us so the sheep don't go anywhere they're not supposed to, like the homestead gardens.'

Harry watched a few sheep that were trotting in front of them. 'They're very dirty sheep.'

'They're merinos. They always look a

bit grubby on the outside, but they've got beautiful white wool underneath. New Zealand produces the best merino wool in the world and this station's famous for their micron count. Under eleven is about as low as it gets.'

'There you go again. Foreign language.'

'Micron count is how fine the wool is. A human hair is about sixty to seventy microns, so that gives you an idea of how fine the wool around here is.'

This time it wasn't a physical skill that impressed Harry. It was her breadth of knowledge. Tilly must have caught what he was thinking as she glanced at his face because she shrugged off any compliment.

'I only know this because my mother started a business in creating high-end merino fabric. And by high end, I mean the best. With her contacts in the fashion industry, she ended up being in huge demand to supply the kind of quality that you see in Armani suits or a Dior coat.'

'That sounds like a high-pressure career.'

'She was always away,' Tilly told him. 'For fashion weeks or photo shoots all over the world. Taking suitcases full of samples and meeting with designers and tailors. She took me to Italy with her on one trip but I hated it. I missed her when she was away, but I missed my pony and my dad too much when I went with her.'

'Your dad didn't go too?'

'No. He adored my mother but he was just as passionate about his work. He's always had a huge sense of responsibility to his patients and community. He still does.'

Harry nodded. 'I can see that. He's going to hate being out of action for as long as it takes for his ankle to heal.'

'I might have to take some more time off and help out until a locum can be found. It's the least I should do after he practically brought me up by himself, even before Mum died.'

'How old were you when you lost your mum?'

'Nine.'

'What happened? Was it sudden?'

Tilly nodded. 'Instant. She had a cerebral aneurysm—at a fashion show in Paris. They said she wouldn't have known anything about it.'

Harry could remember being nine years old. When his mother was by far the most important person in his world and her love had been as sought after as sunshine. Losing her mother like that—not even being anywhere near her when it happened—must have been an incredibly traumatic part of her childhood, but Harry wasn't about to step onto such personal ground by asking any more questions.

'You'd be the perfect locum,' he suggested instead. 'You probably know all his patients as well as he does.'

'Hardly. I left to go to university and I've never been back for more than a few days at a time since then.'

Harry regretted his suggestion as Tilly turned away. He could almost feel shutters coming down and the way she leaned on the horn to scatter the final sheep from the road was the kind of warning signal you might expect from an Ice Queen. This wasn't something she wanted to talk about, was it? And it wasn't any of his business anyway.

So why was he becoming increasingly curious?

Tilly might have had a closer relationship with her father, but had she been hurt by her mother's absence in her early years? Left feeling abandoned at times? Was that part of why her father worried about her being lonely as an adult? And, if she and Jim had such a close bond, why had she been avoiding spending time back here?

Harry could almost see the curling corners of layers to Matilda Dawson, and it was tempting to try peeling them off to discover what was underneath but he knew that wasn't a good idea. Getting too involved with anything—or any*one*—was never a good idea because it inevitably led to tears and even if they weren't his own tears, or if they were symbolic rather than real, Harry had learned it was better to avoid them as much as possible. You kept your distance and, as an insurance policy, you moved on and made a fresh start as often as possible.

It was a relief to distract himself as well as Tilly as they rounded the next bend and then pulled to a halt. He jumped out to open and then close the wide wire gate that would keep the sheep safely enclosed in the 'long acre'. And minutes later they had arrived at their destination.

The sprawling old homestead they arrived at was a hive of activity. A tent was being put up on the front lawn. Several small children, wearing bathing suits, were playing in the spray of a garden sprinkler, shrieking with delight. A man about Harry's age was on a ladder on the veranda, winding long strips of tinsel through the wrought iron lacework.

'Hey… Tilly… I heard you were going to drop in.' He climbed down off the ladder. 'Long time, no see.'

'Hi, Doug. How's it going?'

'Oh…you know.' He was rubbing the back of his neck. 'Kind of crazy, but wonderful. Biggest gathering of the clan we've ever had for Christmas, but knowing it's the last one for Mum is…well…' He cleared his throat. 'We're under instructions to make it the best one ever and apparently that means putting up every Christmas decoration that five generations of Grimshaws have accumulated.'

Doug was giving Harry a curious glance and he wondered how Tilly was going to introduce him, but it seemed that wasn't necessary.

'You must be the boyfriend we've heard about. You're very welcome, mate. I went to school with Tilly, and we all knew she was going to end up being a doctor like her dad.' Doug was smiling as he held out his hand to shake Harry's. 'Knows her own mind, this one. Bit bossy, even…'

Wow…news travelled fast in these parts. Harry caught Tilly's gaze and could read what felt like a confirmation that information was not only widely shared around here but would be a subject of great interest. That there could be repercussions for anything that was seen or heard by others and that Tilly was nervous about an upset that could spoil the next few days. Mainly for her father, he suspected, but also for herself. She might be choosing not to live where she grew up, or even visit very much, but this place— and its people—were important to her.

It didn't even feel as if Harry was acting as he gave her the kind of reassuring, *loving* smile that a couple might share before returning Doug's firm handshake.

'Sometimes bossy can be a very good thing,' he said. 'Tilly's the one you want to be in charge if you're badly injured or sick, that's for sure.'

It was Doug who was smiling at Tilly now. 'I've heard that. You probably don't realise how proud your dad is of you. Come inside. Mum's looking forward to seeing you.' His smile widened. 'And the first man you've ever brought home.'

* * *

The interior of the old homestead had been renovated over the years to create a huge open area of a kitchen and living area—a welcoming space that was full of light. It was also very full of Christmas decorations at the moment. The tip of a real pine tree in one corner touched the high ceiling and was smothered with fairy lights and decorations. The bucket it was anchored into was invisible behind a mountain of brightly wrapped parcels. Tinsel and paper streamers were looped over the rest of the ceiling, numerous stockings were attached to a wide mantelpiece over the fireplace and every available flat surface had some kind of seasonal ornament on it.

The most notable feature of the room, however, was a hospital bed that was positioned so that its occupant had a clear view of the living area, the kitchen and the views of the gardens and mountains from the windows. The bed had silver tinsel wound around the metal framework, a cheerful red blanket and two small children sitting quietly on the end of the bed playing with toys. As Tilly and Harry approached, two teenagers moved closer to gather up the children and

Doug scooped up a toddler from the floor nearby.

'Let's all go outside for a few minutes,' he said, 'and let Dr Tilly talk to Nana.'

Harry had seen Tilly approach all sorts of people in her work environment, patients and colleagues, in all sorts of situations. Even in an emergency—okay, maybe *especially* in an emergency—she always gave the impression of being perfectly calm and in total control. Just the way you'd expect an Ice Queen to behave.

He'd never seen her like this. With tears in her eyes and a wobble in her voice as she reached to hug the woman propped up amongst a cloud of pillows.

'Oh, *Maggie…*'

'If it can't be Jim looking after me, I'm so glad it's you, darling.' Maggie's skin was almost as pale as the white pillows she was resting against but her eyes were bright as she shifted her gaze. 'And you must be Harry. It's another gift for me this Christmas, to know that she's found someone special enough to bring home.'

Oh…*help*…

Suddenly, this game of pretending to be Matilda Dawson's boyfriend for a day or two had become something very different. Something that really mattered to people that Tilly cared about. Something significant.

'It's a privilege to meet you, so it is, Maggie,' Harry said.

'Oh...' Maggie's face lit up with a smile that was directed at Tilly. 'That *accent*... I can see why you fell for him.' She looked back at Harry. 'I had such a crush on Tilly's father when I was at school,' she told him. 'I still had my eye on him after he came back as a newly qualified doctor, but then he met Chiara when she was here for a fashion shoot in the mountains and that was that. Mind you, I could hardly blame him. She was the most beautiful woman I'd ever seen and then she became my best friend...' Maggie paused for breath and then patted Tilly's hand. 'I've got a photo of us in the box over there. I was just sorting them. Can you find it to show Harry?'

It was an old photo. Black and white. It was only Maggie's smile that made her recognisable as one of the young women sitting on a rock beside a lake, but Harry could have sworn that her companion was Tilly. Chiara's dark hair was long and loose, being lifted by a gust of wind, and she seemed to be laughing as she tried to keep it out of her eyes.

And Maggie was right. She was the most beautiful woman *he'd* ever seen as well.

He raised his gaze to Tilly and realised that he'd only ever seen her like this, with her hair scraped back so hard it almost looked like glossy black paint on her skull. If she let it escape from that tight style she could look like her mother's twin. A vibrant, dark angel with no hint of ice anywhere.

Harry listened quietly as Tilly got on with what needed to be done on this visit. She topped up the syringe driver that was delivering a steady dose of narcotics beneath Maggie's skin and she changed the transcutaneous patch that was also part of her pain relief. They talked about how effective the medications for nausea and other symptoms were and whether there was anything else that was needed medically at the moment.

And he kept sneaking more glances at Tilly's face. Imagining her with her hair loose. Taking notice of more than simply her hair. He'd noticed the difference this morning, when he'd seen Tilly wearing clothes other than the baggy scrubs she wore at work, but she'd chosen jeans and a designer sweatshirt to travel in. She'd changed almost as soon as they'd arrived home, and now she was wearing a pair of light cargo pants that ended below the knee and she had a white singlet top beneath a shirt that was mostly unbuttoned. How had he not noticed the generous curve of her breasts on that slim frame? That subtle hint of cleavage, even?

He was seeing the shape of her body in a whole new light as he realised how attractive Tilly actually was.

No… Harry could feel his heart sink as he corrected himself. As he realised how attracted *he* actually was *to* Tilly.

This was definitely not a part of the plan.

Neither was getting emotionally involved. With a family determined to make the most of a last Christmas with a beloved mother and grandmother, or with someone who had ties with this family that were linked to her own, possibly complicated, past.

He could see the tight grip of Maggie and Tilly's hands. He could *feel* the emotion and bond between them.

'I'll be back around the same time tomorrow but don't hesitate to call before then if there's anything bothering you.'

'I'll be fine.'

They all knew that Maggie was not going to be fine but Harry saw the way Tilly followed the older woman's courageous lead. She even found a smile.

'We're off to the pony club party now. I'm filling in for Dad to help judge the fancy-dress competition.'

'I've got two of my grandies there. Look out for Sammy and George. They're twins. Do you remember Doug's older brother, John?'

Tilly nodded. 'Of course. He's got a farm just outside Arrowtown, hasn't he?'

'Yes. But the twins brought their ponies here to get dressed up for the party so I could see them.' Maggie's smile was overly bright. 'They're being Christmas elves and the ponies are reindeer. Nice and easy this time. Do you remember when you won? With your princess costume?'

'You took me,' Tilly said, nodding. 'Mum was away and Dad got called to an accident at the last minute and I was so upset because I thought I wasn't going to be able to go to the party. I remember him ringing you in a panic.'

'He'll be so happy to have you home for

Christmas,' Maggie said. 'Are you staying around a bit longer this time?'

Harry could sense that Tilly was trying to put those shutters up again, the way she had when he'd suggested she could work here as her father's locum. It was obviously harder for her to try and shut Maggie out, however.

'Ah, well...' Maggie reached up to touch Tilly's cheek. 'You'll be back when you're ready, darling. It's your home.' She lay back against her pillows, letting her gaze drift around the room with all its decorations and the smell of Christmas baking. 'We all need to be home in the end,' she said softly.

Both Harry and Tilly were quiet as they drove back through the mob of sheep on the farm's private road. Maybe Tilly was already feeling the grief of losing someone special in her life and he could understand that. All too well. He might be trying to stay uninvolved but maybe it was already too late. And maybe he could offer Tilly a small amount of comfort?

'It's very sad,' he said finally. 'But how lucky is Maggie to be at home with her whole family gathering around her? I was the only family my mam had, and I was too far away when she died.' Harry found himself swallowing hard. 'It's something I'll have to live with but it's made it too hard to go home ever since.'

Tilly didn't speak but her wide-eyed glance said it all. Harry could see surprise that he'd shared something so personal and a connection in that they'd both lost their mothers too soon. It was a glance that only lasted a heartbeat but it gave Harry a glimpse behind the shutters and he could see a child who had lost something she'd never been able to replace. That perhaps she'd never had enough of in the first place? He could feel that vulnerability he'd sensed when he'd wondered if she was lonely and that sense of connection that had hit him like a brick when she'd explained why she had decided to pretend to her father that she was in a serious relationship. After his own revelation when he'd seen that photograph of her mother, there was physical attraction adding a powerful new element to the mix.

Had he really thought he could stay uninvolved?

That ship had already sailed, hadn't it?

And the mix of emotion he was wading through was suddenly enough to make something else seem crystal clear.

'I think Maggie was right,' he added. 'We do all need to be home in the end. I keep going to new places thinking I'm going to find whatever it is I'm looking for and I never do. I think it might be time for me to go home. Perhaps whatever it is, is waiting for me back in Ireland.'

All he could see in Tilly's glance this time was curiosity. 'What is it that you're looking for?'

'I don't know exactly,' Harry admitted. 'I just know there's something missing.'

'Have you ever thought that you might have already found it, but you kept going because you didn't recognise it?'

Harry shook his head. 'I'd know.'

'How?'

Harry shrugged. Then he shook his head to signal an end to a conversation that was getting far too philosophical. 'How are *you* going to know,' he countered, 'who the best dressed-up pony is?'

Tilly threw him a smile. 'I'll know,' she said. 'Because it'll feel right.'

CHAPTER FIVE

THE CRAIG'S GULLY DOMAIN, a ten-acre pad-dock near the lake, bordered by trees that were at least a hundred years old, with its clubrooms, children's playground, tennis courts and a barbecue picnic area was as familiar to Matilda Dawson as the gardens surrounding the home she'd grown up in. Arriving there straight after the visit to Maggie made it feel as if her entire childhood was beginning to fold itself around her like a cloak.

One that felt too heavy. Too hot on this summer's day. Too…suffocating?

She could hear the peal of a child's laughter in the distance, the barking of a dog and the whinny of an overexcited pony. She could see colour everywhere, as both children and their ponies were getting ready for the grand parade and the judging of the fancy-dress costumes. As she and Harry got closer to the picnic area she could even smell the last sausage being taken from the grill to get wrapped in soft bread with a generous splodge of tomato sauce on top.

Good grief…she could almost taste how delicious it was going to be to that hungry child who'd come looking for more food.

The area around the clubrooms was a hive of activity. There were parents tidying up equipment that had been used for games, older riders stacking jumping poles onto a trailer and rolling barrels into the storage space behind the building and other adults who were gathered near one of the big wooden tables that held an urn of hot water, a huge enamel teapot and plates of home-made biscuits and slices.

A chorus of greetings began as soon as they were within earshot.

'Tilly… Merry Christmas! It's so good you could come…'

'How's your dad? We've all heard the news…'

Judging by the looks Harry was receiving, everybody had also heard the news that she'd brought a man home for the first time, which meant that everybody was talking about her. That weighty cloak Tilly had been aware of carrying on her shoulders got a little bit heavier.

'What terrible timing to break his leg right before Christmas...'

'Tilly! It must be ten years since I saw you... You haven't changed a bit.'

That had to be the understatement of the year, Tilly thought, but she recognised an old school and pony club friend just as easily, although Shelley had cut her hair short and had a baby in her arms.

'Would you like a cup of tea? Something to eat?'

'Mrs Patterson.' Tilly turned to the older woman, who really hadn't changed a bit in more than the last decade. 'Are you still the president of the club?'

'Call me Helen, dear. You're all grown up now.' Helen was smiling. 'And no, I haven't been president for a long time, but I'd never miss the Christmas party. I'm always on the judging panel with Jim.'

Tilly was about to introduce Harry to Helen but, as she turned, she could see— and hear—a parent coming towards them, carrying a child who was cradling his arm and sobbing loudly.

'Thank goodness you're here, Tilly,' Helen said. 'We've been missing having Jim as our first aid officer. Looks like Max is our first injury of the day.'

But it wasn't Tilly who got to the child first. It was Harry. She could hear his voice over the miserable crying.

'Is it a plane? Is it a bird? No…it has to be *Superman*…'

The boy was, indeed, wearing a Superman outfit but the excited announcement of his arrival was enough of a surprise to make his cries fade as he stared at Harry instead.

'Max fell off Toby.' His mother sounded worried. 'He's hurt his arm.'

'Are you sure he wasn't flying?' Harry asked. 'Like this?' He held his arms straight in front of him, his head lowered, but he was peeping up at Max.

Tilly saw him wiggle his eyebrows. Max not only stopped crying completely, he giggled.

'Can I see your arm?' Harry asked. 'I know all about flying injuries. Batman came into my hospital once. He'd fallen out of the sky too.'

Max's mother was staring at Harry with an expression very similar to her son's, but there was less tension in her body language. 'Max is upset in case it means he's going to miss the parade.'

'Let's see about that,' Harry said. 'How 'bout we fly you over to the picnic table, Max?'

The small boy seemed happy to be lifted and swooped away to sit on the edge of the picnic table.

'Can you do the secret Superman wave?' Harry had his arms in the air again, this time moving his hands and fingers in gentle spirals.

He could.

'And can I feel those super muscles in your arm?'

Tilly could see how gentle Harry was being as he examined Max's arm and how thorough he was being, despite the unusual approach to an orthopaedic assessment. She could also see the way Max's mother melted under a smile from Harry as he finished, and she could feel herself frowning at the reminder of why she'd never wanted to have anything to do with this good-looking Irishman. Why she'd kept herself safe from falling under that charming spell.

'I don't have my X-ray vision working

today, but I'm happy this isn't an obvious fracture,' he said to Max's mother. 'If we put a nice firm bandage on it, I think Max will be good to go for the parade, but if you notice any swelling or increased pain later on he'll need to be seen again.'

Helen found the first aid box and provided a bandage. She even found a tissue for Max to blow his nose on.

'You go and get ready now,' she told him. 'Maybe Mum can lead Toby in the parade for you so there's no chance of any more bumps.' She turned to Tilly. 'Head out to the middle of the domain and we'll get organised to ride in a big circle around you.' She beamed at Harry. 'And take this gorgeous young man with you. He's clearly an expert on superheroes and probably dragons and elves as well.' She turned away. 'I'll be there in a minute. I've just got to find the box of rosettes and ribbons.'

Harry was nodding but he raised an eyebrow at Tilly as Helen sped off. 'Dragons?'

Tilly pointed as she started walking towards the middle of the large grassy area. 'Over there.'

The pony had a green blanket draped over its body, and there were soft fabric spikes attached to its mane and tail. The rider was wearing a brightly coloured dress and some butterfly wings. There was a unicorn behind her and then a small Shetland pony that was covered in a fluffy white costume to look like a sheep, with her rider dressed as Little Bo Peep.

'There's Maggie's grandies.' Tilly pointed again. 'The matching reindeer and elves.'

The twins' ponies had reindeer antlers attached to their bridles and sleigh bells and tinsel on the reins. Five-year-old Sammy and George had green elf costumes with stripy red and white socks and hats with large plastic ears attached and their father walked between the ponies holding the lead ropes.

'I assumed they were identical twins,' Tilly said. 'I didn't expect one of them to be a girl. Is Sammy a Samantha or George a Georgia?'

'Could be either,' Harry said. 'But it doesn't matter—they're both adorable. Will you look at those smiles?'

But Tilly was looking at Harry. 'You really like kids, don't you?'

'I do.'

'Have you got any of your own?'

He looked startled. 'I'm single,' he told her. 'I thought you knew that.'

'Being single and being a father are not mutually exclusive,' Tilly said. 'And…well… you must know the kind of reputation you have with women.'

For a heartbeat it felt as if Tilly was looking at someone she'd never seen before. Someone who was not only hurt by what she'd said but was somehow deeply disappointed? The impression was gone as instantly as a switch being flicked, however, and the Harry Doyle she was more familiar with was back again as he shrugged.

'What can I do?' he murmured. 'For some inexplicable reason, women seem to fall in love with me with no encouragement.'

Tilly wasn't about to tell him that the reason was actually quite obvious. Or that no more encouragement than one of those smiles was probably needed. Instead, she looked away to where the line of ponies and children was getting rapidly longer.

'Have you never fallen in love back, then?' she asked lightly.

'Why would I do that?' Harry's tone was just as light. 'It might just give me another place I wouldn't want to go back to.'

Like he hadn't wanted to go back to his homeland? Because he didn't want to be reminded of losing his mother? What was that saying about many a true word being spoken in jest? Tilly stole another sideways glance. Somehow the idea of him having been so devastated by losing his mum didn't fit at all with the image of a man who wasn't bothered by any broken hearts he was leaving in his wake.

Helen arrived with the box of ribbons and rosettes and a megaphone and the parade began as ponies and riders began walking in a big circle around the judges.

'They all deserve a prize,' Harry declared.

'Well, we've got enough ribbons,' Helen said. 'We'd just need to come up with enough categories.' With a smile, she handed Harry the megaphone.

Again, here was the Harry that Tilly thought she knew. The confident charmer who could walk into any space and become the centre of attention. The man that every woman wanted to be noticed by. And the fact that he had the ability to dry a child's tears with a performance like the one she'd witnessed when he'd looked after Max would only make him that much more attractive to anyone who was seeking a father for her future children.

It was just as well she wasn't planning on having a family herself, wasn't it?

Harry quickly got into announcing categories and winners. Helen and Tilly attached the ribbons and rosettes to the ponies and congratulated the riders. By the time the adults in the audience realised that every single child was going to be awarded a prize, Harry had won their wholehearted support and the clapping and cheers got more enthusiastic.

'And the prize for the best retro costume—not to mention a reminder that we should all take the time to smell the flowers—are our hippies.'

The pony had peace signs painted on its flanks and a garland of flowers around its neck to match the wreath its rider was wearing along with her fringed vest and flared jeans.

The best nursery rhyme character went to the sheep and Bo Peep and there was an 'African animal' category for the white horse with black zebra stripes and the brown one that had been painted to look like a giraffe.

Maggie's grandchildren were awarded a 'best matching' prize.

Helen made a brief speech thanking all the parents for their support and wishing them all a happy holiday period. She finished by thanking Tilly and Harry for their help with the judging.

'And please tell Jim that the whole club is wishing him a very speedy recovery from his injury,' she finished.

'Yeah...' someone shouted. 'I'm not putting my hand up to clean those barbecues again.'

Tilly was shaking her head as they drove away from the domain a short time later. 'I can't believe Dad still fronts up and cleans those barbecues,' she said. 'I haven't been to a pony club picnic in nearly twenty years. Guess it's one of those small-town things you can never escape if you still live here.'

'Why would you want to?' Harry asked. 'That was one of the best parties I've ever been to. You've already got the pony,' he added. 'You just need a few kids to go with it.'

'Spud's retired.' Tilly didn't want to continue this conversation. 'And I'm no more interested in having kids than you are.'

'I didn't say I wasn't interested,' Harry protested. 'Just that I don't have any. Yet.'

'How many are you thinking of having?'

'Six.' Harry's tone was decisive. 'That way none of them would ever get lonely.'

Tilly laughed out loud but a part of her was imagining Harry with a whole tribe of children and it was making her feel…what… shut out of something important? Like the feeling of coming home she'd had arriving back at the old house tucked into the hills or feeling the warmth of the greetings today from people she hadn't seen for so many years. Like when she'd felt Maggie hugging her back or when she'd seen Shelley with her baby and the man who'd been doing her father's job of cleaning the barbecue.

And there was something else nagging at the back of her mind. Harry had been an only child too. Had he wished for a whole tribe of siblings because of how lonely he'd been himself?

It was tempting to ask but Tilly stopped herself because she had a feeling that she might get another glimpse of the man hiding behind what Harry preferred the world to see. Like seeing the person who'd looked disappointed or hurt, even, by the suggestion he had a reputation that was less than desirable when it came to his relationships with women. Maybe she didn't want to know any more about who the real Harry Doyle might be because there was something here that went far beyond any charm or good looks. Something compelling enough to be disturbing. Something that would draw her too close for comfort.

Fortunately, Harry didn't seem to want to reveal anything else.

'It might never happen,' he said. 'I'm happy the way I am. I love my work.'

'Me too,' Tilly said. 'My career is everything I could have dreamed of, and you can't have that and have kids as well.'

'Some people do.'

'Well, it's not fair on the kids.' Tilly knew she sounded too vehement. Angry, even, so she took a breath and tried to sound like a reasonable adult and not like an unhappy child. 'I'm not going to be the kind of mother who's never there when she's needed. To have kids who know they're not as important as her damn career.'

Harry might be looking out of his side window but she could feel that he was listening to every word.

'My father pretty much brought me up on his own.'

'Looks like he did a good job,' Harry said. 'And he managed to have a career of his own at the same time. I got the impression that he's a much-loved member of this community.'

Tilly blew out a frustrated breath this time. 'I have no desire to end up as a rural GP. Can you imagine how boring that would be after years in a big city emergency department? Treating the same chronic health problems or minor injuries day after day? Anything really interesting or challenging and you'd be referring them to someone else or calling a helicopter to take them away.'

But Harry didn't seem to be listening to her any longer. He was even more focused on the view from his window. 'They work hard around here, these farmers. Will you look at all that hay?'

Huge round bales were dotted over the paddocks they were passing and there were teams of people busy with tractors and other large pieces of machinery.

'It's probably baleage rather than hay.' Tilly was more than happy to move away from discussing anything personal—like

Harry's plans to go back to Ireland and create a big happy family—and go back to her role as a tour guide. 'They look like they're getting ready to wrap the bales in plastic. It's quicker to make because you don't have to leave it to dry so long and it's easier to store. But you're right. They'll be working hard to get it all in while the weather holds. And hoping to get the day off to have Christmas with their families, I expect.'

Yep. This was working well. That disturbing sensation of getting too close to the real Harry was fading fast.

'They'll be making the most of the long summer evenings. It's light enough to work until about ten o'clock at night at the moment.'

It was still more than light, and warm, enough to have dinner outside in the courtyard at the back of the old Dawson villa. Recycled bricks for paving and a lush grapevine growing over a pergola to create a green ceiling gave the area a European vibe, even without the rustic furniture, citrus trees like lemons and mandarins growing in half wine barrels and a generous scattering of candle-holders. A long table and chairs took up one part of the courtyard and there was a seating area around an enormous fire pit on the other side, near a barbecue set up that was more like an outdoor kitchen.

Jim Dawson was sitting in the wheelchair, his moonboot supported by a cushion on the solid wooden bench running the length of the outdoor table, supervising Harry, who was cooking vegetables on a solid grill and about to add some thick slices of fillet steak to the grill over open flames.

'Put Tilly's on first,' Jim directed. 'She likes it incinerated, don't you, love?'

'It's called "well done", Dad.' Tilly put a bowl of fresh green salad on the table beside a basket of bread and smiled at her father as she began arranging cutlery and plates. 'It's good to see you looking a bit brighter.'

'The painkillers are doing a good job.' Jim nodded. 'Plus, I slept most of the afternoon while you were out. I couldn't do much else after I found that all the needles were falling off that old fake tree. I'll test out my crutches when I go and find a real one to chop down in the back paddock after dinner, but I might need some help getting it back to the house.'

'You'll do no such thing,' Tilly said. 'You're allowed to test out your crutches to get around the house when it's absolutely necessary, but that's it. If we see you even trying to put any weight on that leg you'll lose that privilege as well. I'm sure there must be a bedpan amongst that medical museum you've collected out in the barn.'

Harry was grinning broadly. 'I think she's serious, Jim. Don't worry, I'll go and cut down a tree for you.' He was using tongs to turn fried potatoes and mushrooms. 'Let's enjoy dinner first, though. This smells so good.'

'Thanks, lad.' But Jim had caught Tilly's gaze. 'Now, tell me more about how Maggie seemed and how the rest of the family is holding up. And I want to know all about the pony club parade too. It's the first time I've missed it in more than twenty-five years.'

It was Harry who added considerably to Tilly's reports on their afternoon. He wasn't simply a born entertainer, she thought, he was a born storyteller as well. He had them all laughing as he described his terror at seeing a wall of sheep ahead when he had a sheer cliff on his side and again as he role-played the response that people in Ireland might have to ponies and riders dressed up like dragons or elves.

'Sounds more like leprechauns.' His accent was stronger than Tilly had ever heard before. 'Were they as short as our tricksy little fairies? Did you get your three wishes?'

And then he had them all almost in tears as he talked to Jim about Maggie.

'She's in the best place she could possibly be,' he said quietly. 'In the very heart of her family. And in what has to be the most beautiful part of this world I think I've ever seen.'

Jim didn't have any hesitation to ask about things that Tilly was avoiding.

'You must be missing your family, lad,' he said. 'Especially at this time of year.'

'There was only ever my mam,' Harry told him. 'And she died not long after I graduated from medical school. When I was working too many hours to be able to get home for Christmas. But I had it all planned for the next year. I was going to buy the apartment she was living in for her so she'd never have to move again.'

Tilly could see all those years of experience in hearing people's stories etched in the lines of empathy in her father's face but it wasn't hard to feel beneath Harry's words herself. She could hear the loneliness of a small boy and, if she hadn't already been aware of how hard the loss of his only parent had been, she would have heard how much love there had been between them in that desire to protect his mother and keep her safe for the rest of her life. To make her happy, which was pretty much what her motivation had been when she'd lied to her father about Harry.

'So you had to move a lot?' Jim asked.

'We had to go to where Mam could find a new job. Or cheaper rent. I think I went to about fifteen different schools.'

'Not easy,' Jim murmured. 'Being the new kid at school is always scary.'

Harry laughed off what had probably been only a part of a tough childhood. 'Especially when you're the new kid with sticky-out ears. I looked like a wee leprechaun myself, so I did. If I hadn't figured out I could use it to make people laugh, I would have been the most picked-on kid ever.'

So his ability to put on a performance and such a convincing act had come from learning to survive? How much had he been bullied before he'd figured out a way to deflect any attacks? Tilly found herself staring at the tousled waves of dark hair on Harry's head. Did he wear his hair that little bit longer than could be considered neat because he'd learned that it could hide his ears?

Yeah…now that she was looking for it, she could see the outline of Harry's ears quite clearly and the squeeze on her heart was so hard she could feel a part of it cracking. There was something that he must have learned long before he was in control of how long his hair was and that would have been how to protect himself from being picked on by hiding any feelings that would make him seem weaker—like being scared or lonely.

Oh, man…she knew how hard it was to hide feelings like that. And how you had to do it all by yourself because telling someone who you loved the most—like your only parent—would have caused even more pain.

Sometimes, being pulled closer to someone was impossible to predict or resist. The unexpected feeling of a connection with Harry on a level this deep was like something sharp widening that crack in her heart, opening up a place that hadn't seen the light of day for a very long time.

It was so bright it was blinding.

Painful, even. And, weirdly, given that the light was only imaginary, it seemed to be bright enough to be making her eyes water.

* * *

Good grief…

What on earth had possessed him to talk about his childhood like that? To confess the curse of ears that he'd learned to disguise well enough as a teenager by keeping the waves of his hair long enough. He suspected that Tilly's father had seen through his joking about being shifted from pillar to post and bullied at every new school, but maybe it didn't matter that Jim—or Tilly, for that matter—knew more about him than anyone else.

It felt as if it wouldn't make any difference. Not simply because he was only here for a couple of days but because he felt welcome enough to feel at home, both in this wonderful old house but amongst the community the Dawsons were a part of. He hadn't been lying when he'd told Tilly that the pony club picnic had been one of the best parties he'd ever been to. He liked these people. He liked Tilly's father. He wasn't going to think about whether or not he really liked Tilly, however, because that would inevitably remind him of that unsettling physical attraction he'd experienced earlier that afternoon.

Helpfully, Jim was providing a distraction

as he reached for the crutches he'd propped against the end of the table.

'Where are you off to, Dad?' Tilly's tone suggested she was about to order him to sit down again.

'I'm about ready to hit the sack.' he responded. 'It's been quite a day and those pills have knocked me a bit.'

'Don't you want any dessert? I could make a quick fruit salad to have with some ice cream.'

Jim shook his head, but he was smiling. 'Not for me, thanks, love.' He was pushing himself to his feet, with one hand on the edge of the table for balance.

Harry started to get to his feet to help but Jim shook his head again. 'Stay there, son. You've done enough to help for one day. I can manage.'

Tilly followed her father back into the house, watching carefully that he didn't put any weight on his injured leg, but she came back to the courtyard only a short time later.

'It's a good thing the house is all on one level. He's determined to be independent, but I don't think he'll get himself into too much trouble between the bathroom and his bedroom.' She put a bowl onto the table. 'Cheat's dessert,' she admitted. 'But you can't leave Central Otago without tasting some of the stone fruit we're famous for. And it's not Christmastime without cherries.'

Harry reached for a cluster of the plump, bright red cherries as Tilly sat down, but she had the same idea and his fingers touched hers before they found the fruit. That sharp tingle of awareness as his skin touched hers should have been more than enough of a warning but it didn't stop him lifting his gaze as Tilly put a cherry to her mouth moments later and bit into it. Seeing dark red juice staining her lips made that tingle morph into a shaft of a much more intense sensation that came from deep in his belly. This was a warning he couldn't afford to ignore. There was no way he could sit here and watch her eat cherries.

Harry avoided meeting Tilly's gaze so she couldn't know the direction his thoughts were trying to go. He stood up as well, perhaps for the reassurance that he was still in complete control of his body.

'It'll be dark soon,' he said. 'Is there enough time for me to go and cut down that tree your dad wants?'

'Oh… I'd forgotten about that. Yes…' Tilly

got back to her feet. 'We'd better do that, or he might head out with a saw first thing in the morning. I'll just take these plates inside and give them a quick rinse.'

'I'll help.'

Harry picked up Jim's empty plate and then stepped close enough to reach for Tilly's, only she was already reaching to pick up her own plate and, again, their hands touched. This time, it seemed that both of them were shocked by that electric tingle. Plates clattered down onto the table and cutlery jangled onto the bricks below. Harry stooped to gather up the knives and forks and, as he straightened, he noticed two things.

One was that Jim Dawson was standing in the window of a nearby room on the corner of the house, leaning on his crutches as he looked out, probably to enjoy the sight of the fairy lights and candles in this courtyard as the daylight faded. The other was that he'd somehow got a lot closer to Tilly, who had stacked up the plates on the table. She held her hand out for the cutlery.

'I can see your dad at a window,' he said. 'In the room under the turret.'

'That's his bedroom. That's where he's supposed to be.'

Tilly had wrapped her fingers around the cutlery handles, but Harry didn't let go. 'If I can see him, he can see us.'

Tilly wasn't letting go of the cutlery either. And now her gaze was holding his just as tightly. He saw the tip of her tongue emerge to touch her lips.

'So…?'

'So maybe we should give him something more interesting to see…?'

He could see the instant that Tilly understood what he was suggesting. And, despite the fading light and the dark brown colour of her eyes, he was sure he could see her pupils dilating enough to signal that she not only understood, she was up for it.

And maybe it had nothing to do with trying to put on a convincing performance of being a loved-up couple for her father.

Maybe Tilly wanted it as much as he suddenly did?

They were both still holding that damned cutlery as he bent his head to touch her lips with his own, but Harry found himself letting go as the astonishment of that first contact hit home. He needed a hand to cup the back of Tilly's head and make sure it didn't move while he took a moment to find out whether a kiss could really feel so totally different to anything he'd ever experienced before.

He discovered that it could about the same time he heard that cutlery hitting the paving again.

He could feel Tilly melting in his arms, which suggested she was under the power of the same spell he was experiencing, so then he needed his other hand to trace the line of her spine, feeling each little bump until he reached the roundness of her buttocks. Now he could support her whole body. He could also pull it a little closer to his own as he fell further into that extraordinary kiss and let his tongue explore the delicious taste of her more thoroughly.

It was when the tip of his tongue touched Tilly's that it happened.

A change as sudden as a physical blow that came from nowhere as every muscle in Tilly's body tensed so fast it felt as if someone had waved a wand and turned her to stone.

Instinctively Harry jerked back and that

was when he could see an expression in her eyes that sent a chill rippling down his spine.

Tilly looked…

Dear Lord…was she frightened? Of *him*?

It was a moment of utter confusion. What on earth had made her react to a kiss like this? Or should the question be *who*, not what?

Harry didn't get time to process the implications of that thought because he could hear Tilly's name being called. Urgently. As if her father was aware of her reaction even though he'd been too far away to see it, and that was beyond strange as well.

Tilly was turning to the window her father must have just opened.

'What's wrong?'

Harry could see that Jim had a phone in his hand. 'It's not me. There's been an accident. Down on the Marshalls' farm, near the domain. They need help. Fast.'

Tilly was already moving quickly, and Harry was right behind her. 'Do you know what's happened?' he called back to Jim.

'It sounds bad.' Jim sounded upset. 'Take my truck—it's got all the gear locked in the back tray and you're going to need it. There's an ambulance on the way from Queenstown but you'll get there first.' His voice cracked. 'And they're not likely to have a field amputation kit if it's needed. Someone's got themselves caught in a hay baler.'

CHAPTER SIX

FLIGHT.

Fight.

Or freeze.

Tilly was perfectly well aware of the physiological reaction the body had to an acutely stressful event, like the imminent threat of an attack that could involve personal harm or possible death.

She'd never experienced all three responses in such close proximity, however.

She had almost felt the initial flood of hormones being released as her body had frozen the instant she'd felt the touch of Harry's tongue against her own. She'd been aware of her heart rate increasing so suddenly and she'd known she was probably as white as a sheet by the time Harry had pulled back to stare at her because she'd actually felt the blood draining from her face.

He couldn't have missed the fact that something was wrong but, in the space of only a heartbeat, Tilly had the horrible impression that Harry knew *what* was wrong. The last thing she wanted was to discover that he had guessed a truth she'd been successfully hiding for years so she'd gone from being frozen to being ready to take flight.

Maybe she wouldn't have actually run away from him but there were other ways of creating a safe distance. Like putting up barriers. Refusing to discuss something. Making absolutely sure that he couldn't touch her again—even though, moments ago—it had been the thing she'd wanted more than anything else imaginable.

But she didn't have to do any of those things because of her father's interruption and the call to an emergency that meant she was needed to join the fight for someone's life. If they *were* still alive by the time they got to the scene. Tilly had heard of horrific accidents involving farm machinery like hay balers and she knew there was a real chance that, no matter how fast Harry was driving, they might be too late. She was still ready for a fight, with her heart rate and breathing a lot faster than normal and her muscles tense, but Tilly was relieved that the trembling of her hands was receding.

Harry had noticed that when she'd unlocked the hard cover of the back of the ute to check that all her father's emergency medical supplies were in there. She'd been fumbling with the keys and had offered no resistance when he took them from her hand and told her he'd drive.

And here they were, speeding along the open road with the magnetic light on the roof of the vehicle flashing red against an increasingly deep twilight. The levels of catecholamines like adrenaline that Tilly still had circulating had to be responsible for her astonishingly heightened awareness of every one of her senses. She could see the flash of red light catching the lamp-posts as they sped past, feel every bump in the road and hear the pounding of her own heart in her ears. She could smell freshly cut hay through the open window and she could… oh, dammit…she could still taste Harry's kiss, couldn't she?

She should have known it would have ended like that.

That it was impossible to go any further… No matter how desperately she had wanted it to. It was the first time she'd felt like that since…since…

No…she couldn't think about that. The memory might be trying to surface but it couldn't be allowed. Especially not right now…

'Talk to me.' To Tilly's relief, Harry's voice cut off her train of thought with the precision of a guillotine. 'What relevant gear have we got?'

'Intubation and surgical airway kit. Combat tourniquet. IV gear and fluids. Amputation kit with scalpels, a Gigli saw and sutures.'

'Drugs?'

'Ketamine, fentanyl, midazolam, morphine…' Tilly rattled off a list of drugs she knew her father would have available as a first responder. 'The drug kit's a locked toolbox and the key's on the same key ring as the rest. From memory, it's got a blob of red paint on it.'

'Defibrillator?' Harry wasn't taking his eyes off the road as he steered around a curve, retracing the route they'd taken not that long ago on their way home from the pony club event. 'Portable ventilator? Handheld ultrasound device?'

'Only a defib. I'm not sure that the ambulance carries a portable ventilator or ultrasound either, but I know air rescue does and there may already be a helicopter on the way.' Tilly leaned forward as if it would help her see further. 'We're almost there. I can see a fire truck in the paddock, so our local volunteers are on scene.'

'Good. I don't know much about hay balers, but if someone's trapped in a machine we're likely to need some extrication expertise.' Harry was slowing the ute to turn into the gate and Tilly heard him swear under his breath.

'He's alive,' he said grimly. 'I can hear him screaming from here.'

The sound of someone in extreme pain was unnerving and there were several distressed-looking people, who weren't part of the fire service crew, around the tractor and trailer unit. One man had his arms around the waist of a person who seemed to be leaning right inside the hay baling machine, his feet just off ground level, which made it more difficult for Harry and Tilly to get close enough to assess the scene.

'I can't let go,' he told them. 'If I do, and

Jase falls backwards, he might rip his whole arm off.'

'Get me *out*...' There was another shriek of pain from the man they couldn't see.

'How did this happen?' Harry's tone was clipped.

'I didn't see it. I just found him like this. He said something was wrong with the net that gets fed out to wrap the bale, so he opened the flap to have a look. He knew not to lean in too close, but he got his hand tangled and it just sucked him in.'

'Is everything turned off?'

'Yep.' The affirmation came from one of the volunteer fire officers. 'And, as far as we can tell, Jase's arm has somehow gone down past the cutters and he's been spiked with the pick-up rake. We're getting some gear ready to see if we can cut in from the front. The ambulance isn't far away and there's a chopper on the way from Dunedin that's just taken off.'

Harry climbed onto a wheel. 'Hey Jase? My name's Harry. I'm a doctor. I've got another doctor with me and there's an ambulance on the way. We're going to get you out of here, okay?' He looked over his shoulder. 'Has someone got a torch?'

Tilly heard another heartrending groan from the victim. 'It hurts, man,' he said to Harry. 'It hurts so bad…'

'I know, mate. We're going to give you something to help with that. I'm just trying to see what's going on. It's your left arm that's trapped, yes?'

'It's got spiked…right up to my elbow.' Jase's voice was shaking. 'Oh, God…you're going to cut my arm off, aren't you?'

'I'm only holding a torch, mate.' Harry's tone was one of reassurance. 'Just having a look. Your right arm's not injured, is it?'

'I can't feel my fingers now. I've been hanging on hard to something in there, so I didn't fall. I don't feel good, man… I'm kinda dizzy…'

Tilly had the drug kit open on the back of the ute, pulling out the ampoules of the heavy-duty painkillers they were going to need. The problem was going to be not only getting the access to administer them but keeping their patient safe if he lost consciousness which would become more of a risk after administering medications like these.

But a quick sideways glance showed Tilly the vicious metal spikes attached to the rake mechanism. If this farmer's arm was impaled by them right up to his elbow and his own weight was putting pressure on the limb, it was no wonder he was in so much pain and making this even a little more bearable was a top priority. She knew Harry would be trying to assess vital signs, to record how well Jase was breathing and to estimate his blood pressure and how well oxygen was being circulated.

Wait… *Jase?*

Tilly turned to the nearest fire officer. 'Is this Jason Marshall?' she asked. 'About thirty-four years old?'

'Sure is. You know him?'

'I went to school with him.'

Harry had climbed down in time to hear her, and his gaze focused sharply on her face. 'You okay?'

She nodded as a response. It might be a rare thing to be personally acquainted with a patient who turned up in an urban emergency department, but it was something that happened all the time in a rural situation. 'How's he looking?'

'His airway's clear but he's tachypnoeic at thirty breaths a minute and tachycardic at well over a hundred beats a minute. I can't reach in far enough to assess injuries or the degree of entrapment but his left arm's pulled so far in, the shoulder's almost dislocating, which will only be adding to his pain levels. I couldn't try to get a radial pulse on his un-injured arm to get an idea of blood pressure because he's too scared to let go of whatever he's holding to support himself.'

'We need to get IV access to give him some pain relief. Or intraosseus if we can only reach his leg? I want to get fluids running. Oxygen on. And a cardiac monitor as soon as we can.'

'We need a better platform to support him. If he crashes, we could well be looking at having to do an amputation just to get access to intubate. I'm going to talk to the firies.'

Tilly added the syringes she'd filled to an IV roll, fastened it and then pulled on a pair of gloves. 'I'll climb up and have a look. I'm a lot smaller than you and I might be able to reach further.'

Harry frowned. 'Be very careful where you're putting your own hands. If anything moves—the patient or the machinery—you could end up trapped yourself and the last thing we need is another patient.'

'I know that.'

The noise and activity around her was increasing steadily as Tilly found a foothold on a metal bar of the hay baler and started talking to their patient as she leaned in.

'Hey, Jase...you probably won't remember me but we went to school together. Tilly Dawson? My dad's been the GP in Craig's Gully for ever.'

'Tilly...yeah... I remember... What the heck are you doing here?'

'I came down to visit Dad for Christmas. And I took this call because I'm a doctor now too.' Tilly shone the torch to follow the line of the trapped arm but couldn't see past a roller with sharp-looking blades. 'I'm an emergency medicine specialist.'

'Oh, yeah... I heard something about that.' Jason's voice was getting weaker and the cry of pain he uttered was quieter but no less agonised. 'Help me...' he groaned. *Please...*

'I'd like to get a line into your good arm. That'll be the fastest way to deal with your pain.' Tilly could reach Jason's uninjured arm, but his elbow was sharply bent and the muscles locked. 'Can you try and let go with this hand?'

'No...' Jason sounded terrified. 'I'll fall...'

Floodlights were being set up beside Tilly

and she could hear sirens getting louder as both an ambulance and a police car arrived on scene. She could hear Harry's voice sounding calm as he asked quick-fire questions about the approach being planned to try and free the trapped limb and directed people to different tasks, including finding something solid to get beneath Jason's feet. She knew the man supporting Jason would be getting tired enough to need replacing but she didn't expect it to be Harry who wrapped his arms around Jason's chest.

'I've got you, mate,' he said. 'I'm not going to let you fall.'

Tilly could actually feel the rumble of Harry's voice as much as she could hear it, because it seemed to go from her ears right down to her bones. If she was terrified or in pain, she thought, that deep, calm voice and the promise in his words would be exactly what she needed to hear. She could, in fact, imagine putting her life in Harry Doyle's hands with no hesitation at all.

'You can let go now, Jase,' Harry added. 'You're safe. And Tilly needs that arm so we can help you with that pain as fast as possible.'

Jason was sobbing but he did let go and it

was reassuring to be able to assess the radial pulse she could feel in his uninjured wrist and find it was strong enough to suggest that Jason hadn't yet lost a dangerous amount of blood. Harry held him as Tilly juggled her supplies to get a tourniquet around the arm and a wide bore cannula slipped into a vein and then secured firmly with tape. And then she could finally administer drugs that were going to deal with the pain and terror that this young farmer was suffering.

Tilly could hear the sound of the rescue helicopter arriving as she felt Jason's body relaxing as his pain receded. Harry was calling for more help in supporting the weight of their patient and then he moved himself, climbing up so that he was right beside Tilly.

'I'll hold him from this side,' he said. 'Can you get on the wheel and see if you can feel what's going on with his other arm? It would be good to know how long it might be before we'll be able to get him down to ground level.'

This was a lot scarier than the challenge of gaining IV access. Tilly had to slide her hand past those sharp blades, following the line of Jason's arm into a dark space. Within seconds, she could feel the end of one of the spikes that were there to gather and move hay from the ground. It was right through Jason's arm, just below the elbow. There was more space in this part of the machinery, so Tilly stood on tiptoes and leaned in a little further. She wanted to reach his wrist, to feel for a pulse and then his hand to make sure it was still intact after having gone past those blades. Her face was very close to Jason's now.

'You had long hair.' His words were slightly muffled, as if it was an effort to speak. He didn't seem to be aware of what was happening around him. 'I tied your plaits together when I was sitting behind you...'

Harry was just as close to Jason on the other side so she could hear his chuckle. 'Sounds like you were the class clown,' he said. 'Like me.'

Tilly could feel another spike that was very close to Jason's wrist. Or was it angled up through his palm? Was it anywhere near the artery? Could that metal tubing cause potentially fatal blood loss if it moved during an extrication attempt?

'I seem to remember him sticking a whole bunch of pencils through them once,' Tilly said aloud. 'And everybody laughed at me when I got up.'

She was gently exploring Jason's hand as she spoke. The metal prong felt like it was involving several fingers.

'Don't try moving them,' she said, 'but can you feel me touching your fingers? Here? And here?'

'Yeah...'

'How's the pain level, mate?' Harry asked. 'On a scale of zero to ten with zero being no pain and ten the worst you can imagine?'

'Dunno...' Jason sounded sleepy. 'Maybe six...?'

'And what was it when we arrived?'

Jason gave a huff of sound almost like laughter. 'Bloody twenty-six, mate...'

'Good to know. We'll keep you topped up so it won't ever get that bad again.' Harry was watching Tilly as she lifted her head. 'I'm going to get someone else to come and hold you for a bit. Maybe someone on both sides. Tilly and I need to talk to the experts and decide on the quickest and safest way to get you out of this.'

'I need to get home,' Jason mumbled. 'I've got kids, you know? And it's nearly Christmas...'

With the helicopter crew now on the ground they were able to join the discussion of how best to manage both the extrication and medical management for Jason. It was an intense exchange of expertise with factors to consider such as the danger of a respiratory arrest from the powerful analgesic drugs and the vibration that could make the injuries worse with hydraulic tools being used to cut into the metal of the farm machinery.

Of all the medics present, Tilly was the only one small enough to be able to reach Jason's impaled arm and it was her own idea to try and support the limb as they gained access. That way they would know if the vibration and manipulation of the metal could be creating additional issues and the fire officers could change to using an oxy acetylene torch, which might be slower but would cause far less vibration. Tilly's ability to reach Jason's arm would be even more important in that case, because she would need to protect his arm, with water-soaked dressings, from heat transfer that could cause severe burns.

And, of all the rescue people present, the only person Tilly wanted right beside her during this next phase, the one responsible for supporting Jason's body weight, was Harry. Because she could only do this if she could trust that she wasn't going to be suddenly jolted by the weight of Jason's body shifting. It was still surprisingly easy to trust Harry because she could still hear the echoes of his voice reassuring Jason.

'I've got you, mate... You're safe...'

Harry had never been in a situation quite like this.

He was acutely aware of everything happening around him—the noise of the pneumatic gear, every bump or shudder in the metal framework of the machinery he was leaning against, even anybody walking past who might be close enough to interfere with his task of keeping Jason's body as still as possible.

Should he have tried to talk Tilly out of putting herself at risk by having her own arm inside that machine as they tried to dismantle it? If Harry could have taken her place he would have, in a heartbeat, but all he could do now was his absolute best to keep Tilly as safe as possible. And applaud her, silently, for her courage as the rescue workers worked, slowly and carefully, to get him free.

The farmer who'd raised the alarm had a toolbox in his truck so some machinery parts could be unbolted and prised free. The 'Jaws of Life' cutter and spreader took care of other barriers to get in to where Jason's arm was impaled but each step was being taken with the utmost caution.

Harry was not only focused on keeping Tilly safe, he was doing his best to both distract and reassure Jason as well as watching for any warning of him losing consciousness or going into respiratory or cardiac arrest.

Tilly was clearly thinking along the same lines.

'I can't believe you're a dad, Jase,' she said at one point. 'Doesn't seem that long since we were at school.'

'I've got three... Oldest is nearly five... she's so excited about Christmas...'

'I'll bet she is,' Harry said. 'What's she asked Father Christmas for?'

'She won't tell me. She'll only tell Santa... Hey...isn't it your dad, Tilly, who does that?'

'Don't spread it around,' Tilly told him. 'But it's going to be Harry this time. Father

Christmas with an Irish accent. We'll have to see how that goes.'

'Ireland's closer to the North Pole than New Zealand,' Harry protested. 'It'll be all good. And Jase? I promise I'll let you know what it is she's set her wee heart on. With a bit of luck you might have it already wrapped up and under the tree.'

Jason made a sound that was almost laughter. 'Hope not... We've got her a pony...'

'Oh...she's going to be so excited. I've still got my first pony, Spud. He's really old now but I still love him to bits. You're close to the pony club grounds so that'll be handy.' Tilly was doing her best to keep Jason distracted. 'How big is the pony you've got?'

'Not big. He's a Shetland.'

'What colour?'

'Sort of yellow, I guess. With a white mane and tail.'

'A palomino. My favourite colour. What's his name?'

'Pudding.'

Tilly laughed. 'That's a great name. Is he nice and quiet?'

'Bombproof, they said.'

'Sounds perfect.'

When exterior sections of the machine had

been cut clear and the rake was exposed, they had to switch to the oxy acetylene torch. Wads of gauze soaked in saline were passed up to Tilly, who covered the exposed skin on Jason's arm around each of the protruding spikes so that they could be separated from the reel. She put goggles on to protect his eyes and wore a pair herself and they tucked the edges of a burn blanket into gaps for extra protection.

When Jason was finally lifted clear he went straight into the skilled care of the air rescue team. They assessed his vital signs, hooked him up to monitoring equipment and topped up his pain relief and then padded and bandaged the impaled spikes to make sure they weren't going to move en route. The team was so efficient, it felt like only minutes later that Harry and Tilly were standing in the paddock, watching the helicopter take off. Sharing a glance that was like a huge sigh of relief.

'That could have been so much worse,' Harry said. 'He needs urgent surgery to remove those spikes but I don't think there's any danger of him losing his arm.'

'He might not even lose any of its function,' Tilly agreed. 'But he could have lost his life.'

'I'd better remember that promise, hadn't I? Except…how will I recognise his daughter? I don't even know her name.'

'I'll ask Dad. He'll know.'

The ambulance from Queenstown was heading off to another job. The fire crew were packing up their tools. The helicopter was nothing more than a tiny flashing light far enough away to be one of the stars.

'What was that you were saying?' Harry asked as they packed away their own kit into the back of the ute. 'About it being so boring being a rural GP?'

Tilly made a huff of sound. 'That's not the kind of job that happens every day. But it is another reason I wouldn't want to be one. You know all your patients. You went to school with them, or you see them in the supermarket when you're getting your groceries.'

'I guess that would kind of blur the lines between your professional and personal life,' Harry agreed. 'But there's another side to that coin, isn't there?'

Tilly's glance was suspicious.

'Doesn't it make it feel more like they're

real people and not just statistics in the throughput of an ED? That you're a significant person in their lives?'

'It means you can end up knowing things about their lives or their bodies that you can't tell anybody else and…and I don't really like keeping secrets.'

'So it makes a whole community a bit like a family, huh?' Harry held the passenger door open. 'I'll drive back, shall I?'

'Thanks.' Tilly nodded. 'I'm a bit wrecked, to be honest.' She leaned back against the headrest as he began to drive them home and closed her eyes. 'I must have used way too much adrenaline in the last couple of hours.'

It was only then that Harry remembered what had happened moments before they'd responded to that emergency call. The fear he'd seen in Tilly's eyes.

Whatever had caused that reaction was none of his business, was it?

He didn't want to get involved with Tilly's life, did he?

Harry drove in silence for several minutes.

He was already involved, wasn't he?

And it was his business. Because…what if he'd caused that fear?

Their headlights made a yellow arrow-shaped signpost glow just ahead of them and Harry braked sharply enough for Tilly's eyes to snap open as she sat up straight.

'What are you doing?'

'That signpost said this is Craig's Lake.' The four-wheel drive vehicle was bouncing over potholes on a shingle road. 'I'd like to see it.'

'It's not that spectacular,' Tilly said. 'More like a big pond, really.'

It was big enough to have a grassy area to park on, picnic tables to wander past and a pebbled beach where you could stand and admire the moonlight on water that was still enough to be reflecting the dark shapes of the surrounding hills.

It was Harry who broke a silence that felt deeper than this small lake probably was.

'Was it something *I* did,' he asked Tilly quietly, 'that scared you? Did I make a mistake in thinking you wanted me to kiss you?'

He heard the way Tilly sucked in her breath. She hadn't expected this. She didn't want it.

Harry didn't break the silence this time. He simply waited. He could sense that she was struggling with whether to say anything or not and if she chose not to he would respect her boundaries. He was about to suggest they went home when she did finally speak.

'It wasn't your fault,' she whispered. 'It was mine.'

To his horror, Harry saw a fat tear escape Tilly's eye and trickle down the side of her nose.

Oh, no…what had he done now? The Ice Queen was melting.

There was something so heartbreaking in both Tilly's words and that sad single tear that there was only one thing Harry could do now.

He folded Tilly into his arms.

And simply held her.

CHAPTER SEVEN

THIS SHOULD HAVE been mortifying.

Tilly knew perfectly well that she had a reputation for being aloof at work. Uninterested in gossip, even less interested in any attention from male colleagues. She suspected nobody particularly liked her but that didn't bother her too much because she knew that everybody respected her. They knew how good she was at her job and they knew she could handle anything without falling apart or making stupid mistakes.

If it became public knowledge that she was capable of falling apart to the extent that she was sobbing in Harry's arms it would be just as embarrassing as anybody finding out she'd pretended that she was in a relationship with him. But Tilly wasn't even thinking about something like that happening. She knew it wouldn't, in fact, because she knew that she could trust Harry Doyle.

She'd pretty much been trusting him with her safety for more than the last hour or so and she'd done that with the conviction that she would be quite prepared to trust him with her life. So maybe that was why—for the first time in at least ten years—Tilly was letting herself experience an emotional release.

Because she felt *this* safe…

Turning off the tears turned out to be a bit harder than letting them escape. At some point Harry had got them both sitting on the pebbles of the lake shore but that must have been a while ago because, by the time Tilly noticed, Harry's shirt was soaked. She found herself dusting it with her hand in the forlorn hope it might dry it off.

'Sorry…'

Harry still had his arm around her and he gave her a squeeze. 'I'm not bothered,' he said. 'It's probably warm enough to go swimming, and if I did that my shirt would get a whole lot wetter than this. Unless I went skinny-dipping, of course.'

Tilly made a strangled sound, halfway

between a sob and laughter and that made Harry smile.

'That's better. Now…are you ready to talk to me?' He still hadn't taken his arm away. 'I'd still like to be sure that this wasn't my fault. Because I'm already quite sure it wasn't yours.'

Tilly knew that if she moved from where she was leaning against Harry's body, with her head tucked in under his collarbone, he would lift his arm instantly. So she kept very still.

'It was,' she said quietly. 'I'm…um…different from most people.'

'I already knew that.' She could hear the smile in Harry's tone. 'That's not necessarily a bad thing, you know.'

'It is when you're… When you can't…'

The words died on Tilly's tongue as she turned her face into Harry's damp shirt. How could she possibly say it out loud? Especially to someone like Harry who was so gorgeous and had probably already lost count of how many women he'd made love to. No wonder they were lining up hopefully, like that young nurse, Charlotte. If he could *kiss* like that, imagine how it would feel to go further. All the way…

Maybe it was the fatigue of having depleted her adrenaline levels, both with her reaction to Harry's kiss and then the intensity of the rescue scene they'd both been so involved with. Maybe it was the feeling of safety Tilly had found in Harry's company. In his touch. Or maybe it was simply that she was over dealing with this entirely by herself because it was too lonely. Hopeless, even. She'd never know what it was like to be made love to by someone like Harry...

'When you can't do sex,' she heard herself whispering into the darkness. 'Because you're frigid...'

Who knew that it was possible to communicate incredulity without making a sound? It was the way Harry's muscles tensed. The way she found he was looking at her when she lifted her gaze. The huff of sound he made finally that was like an exclamation point.

'You're *serious*...'

Tilly didn't say anything. Because there was nothing more to say?

Harry blew out a breath. 'How do you know?' he asked.

'I just do.'

'Uh-uh… I'm not buying that.' Harry was watching her. 'I kissed you not so long ago, in case you've forgotten. There's a lot you can tell about someone when you kiss them.'

Every disparaging thought Tilly had ever had about how much Harry would know about sex because he was such a player and didn't actually care about all the women he played with evaporated in that instant. He *did* care. And perhaps he *could* read what was going on in a woman's head when he was kissing her.

Oh…dear Lord…

But Harry's voice was softening. Gentle now. 'You got scared, didn't you?'

Still Tilly said nothing.

Now Harry's voice had a grim edge to it. 'Did the person who scared you happen to be the same person who suggested that you were frigid?'

This time Tilly's silence was broken by Harry's curse.

'Is it someone who lives around here? Is that why you don't like coming home? Just tell me who he is, sweetheart, and I'll go and punch his lights out.'

The sound Tilly made this time was much

closer to laughter than a sob but she could feel something soft and warm blossoming deep inside.

Harry was angry about what had happened to her.

And he'd called her *sweetheart*… Like her father did. Only it didn't feel remotely like the way it did when her father said it.

'He doesn't live around here,' she said. 'But I guess it was part of the reason I stayed away. Why I didn't say anything. To anyone. I couldn't bear it if my father knew. Or anybody else, because that's what this place is like. Everybody knows everything and I'd always be the girl who went to university and was stupid enough to get herself…'

She couldn't say the word.

But Harry could. *'Raped…?'*

He swore under his breath at the way Tilly cringed, which confirmed his guess. This was worse than he'd thought. He'd been imagining that some bastard had tried it on and accused Tilly of being frigid because she'd refused to go to bed with him. But he'd bullied or *forced* her to have sex with him after she'd made it clear she didn't want to?

Harry was aware of several emotions vying for supremacy.

Anger that this had happened to her. So much anger it could tip into rage with very little additional provocation.

He was also filled with an empathy for Tilly that made him want to hold her close again and offer some kind of comfort.

But there was shame in the mix too...for ever having thought of her as being an 'Ice Queen' without even considering that there might be a story behind the way she presented herself to the world. Or, rather, hid from it? A horrible, heartbreaking story.

'Oh, my God, Tilly,' he said slowly. 'Did you report him? Did you get help to deal with it?'

That shake of Tilly's head wasn't a surprise. Harry had already guessed that she'd kept this hidden. That she'd dealt with it herself by pushing it aside. Bottling it up. Good grief...the kind of damage that could cause was appalling.

'I couldn't,' Tilly whispered. 'Because it was my fault... I'd gone out with him. I wanted it to happen but...but not like that. I wasn't ready but he said I'd led him on. That if I stopped being such a prude I'd end up liking it as much as everybody else did. He said…'

'*He* said?' Harry broke into her hesitant speech. 'He made you believe that it was somehow *your* fault? You were gaslighted, Tilly. You do realise that, don't you?'

Tilly's shrug had a tone of despair. 'He said that if I told anybody he'd make sure everybody knew that I was frigid…that I was a waste of time as a woman and no one would ever want to touch me. There were people at uni who knew people from around here. And everybody around here knew my mother, who was the most beautiful, *sensual* woman they'd ever seen. The word most people used about my mum was passionate, and they might have meant about her career but we all knew they really meant more than that. I heard men say more than once that my dad was a *very* lucky man.'

'Tilly…' Harry was shaking his head. 'When Maggie showed me that photo of your mother today, I thought it was *you*. That if you untied your hair you'd look like your mum's twin.'

'As if…' It was Tilly's turn to shake her head. 'I was the gawkiest kid. I was too skinny and kind of clumsy. I had awful hand-eye co-ordination. Riding my pony was the only sport I was ever good at.'

'Did your ears stick out?' Harry lifted his hair with his thumbs to expose his ears and made a face at the same time. He knew he was reverting to that emotional escape he'd perfected so long ago, by being the class clown, but he hadn't known that it could still work just as well—and for other people as well as himself.

Because, to his delight, Tilly actually laughed. 'You *do* look like a leprechaun,' she said.

Harry let his hair fall and straightened his face. And then he waited a beat to let any echoes of joking dissipate.

'And you look like an astonishingly beautiful woman,' he said quietly. 'I couldn't see past the wall you put up because you do a good job of not letting the world see who you really are. Maybe I couldn't see a reason to try.' His smile was gentle. 'You can be quite intimidating, you know, Dr Dawson. You keep people at more than arm's length.'

Tilly was looking down, playing with a pebble she'd picked up from the beach. 'I guess it was safer. And then it just became normal and it didn't really matter any longer because I love m1y job so much.'

Harry watched her hand close around that pebble and hold it. He knew it still mattered. Tilly was missing out on a huge part of life. Wiping out an entire future for herself. Staying away from an incredible part of the world that she clearly loved had also become normal, hadn't it? No wonder her father had been worried about her. He must have seen the changes in his daughter as she'd distanced herself but would have had no idea why.

The saddest thing was that, with the right help, it should have been possible for Tilly to have been able to move on without losing so much of her life. Maybe it was *still* possible, but Harry couldn't think of what he could say to open a conversation like that. Or what he could do to help her, other than to try and make her laugh.

'You know what?' Harry made it sound as if he was about to change the subject. Or suggest that it was time they headed home?

'What?'

'You're a great kisser.'

The stone dropped from Tilly's hand as her head jerked up, her jaw dropping. He held her gaze for a long, long moment. When he spoke again, his voice was as quiet and still as the moonlit lake in front of them.

'You can trust me, Tilly. You know that, don't you?'

She nodded slowly but he could see that trust in her eyes. He knew it had quite a lot to do with the tense rescue scene they'd just completed together where she'd had to trust him to help keep her safe, but this wasn't about any professional relationship they might have. It very clearly went a lot deeper than that or Tilly would never have told him something she'd kept secret for so long.

'And you can tell me anything at all and it won't go any further. I quite like keeping secrets, me.'

He could see something added to that trust now. Appreciation, perhaps, that not only had he heard something she'd said to him a while ago, he understood how hard it must have been to keep her own terrible secret.

'You should also know,' he added, 'that I'd never, ever do anything you didn't want me to do.'

Again, Tilly nodded. Even more slowly. As though she was thinking carefully about what he'd said. As though she was thinking there *might* be something she would want him to do?

'I wish I could show you how wrong you are to believe that you're frigid. I wish that I knew how to erase that fear you've built up over far too long.'

Oh…there was a thought.

Maybe he did know how he could help her do that. If he was gentle enough and patient enough—if Tilly would let him, he could show her at least a part of what she was missing out on. And that could change her life, which would be…

Possibly the best gift anyone could give Matilda Dawson?

Not that he could wrap it up, mind you. Or offer a voucher. He couldn't even put it into words without it sounding…what…weird? Sleazy, even?

He could let himself think about it, though. To tap into how attracted he was to Tilly and how easily that could spark desire. He could imagine kissing her again and how it could lead to something more, and maybe she would be able to see everything he couldn't say aloud as he continued to hold her gaze.

It was Christmas, after all. What better time to offer a gift?

* * *

It was an odd thing, this feeling of being so safe with someone.

As if the child she had once been, so long ago, was peeping out from a hiding place in her head—or her heart—that had been so effective Tilly had almost forgotten that little girl she had once been still existed somewhere deep inside. She could still feel that kind of safety that came from being tucked up, snuggled into bed or onto the couch beside her daddy, knowing that he would read her favourite story until she was sound asleep.

Even more oddly, it made Tilly yawn. A deep, whole-body stretching kind of yawn, filling her lungs with the cool night air and ending with an audible sigh.

Except Harry didn't seem to think it was odd.

'Come on… I'm not surprised you're exhausted.' He got to his feet and held out his hand to help her up. 'It's been one hell of a day, so it has.'

Tilly let him take her hand and pull her up. A strong, warm grip that made her feel as safe as everything else about this man.

It seemed impossible that she'd met him

at the airport only this morning as no more than an acquaintance. A work colleague who was doing her a favour because he felt that he owed her something or it just suited him to be out of town for Christmas. Now, it felt as if she'd known Harry for ever.

In fact, she'd never felt quite like this before. Ever. The scientific part of her brain suggested that it might be due to hormone depletion after the adrenaline-filled hours she'd just experienced. Simple fatigue might have been enough on its own. Or it could be a psychological effect of having talked about the incident that she knew perfectly well had left her with a degree of PTSD.

A far less scientific explanation was coming from the feeling that seemed to be centred around her heart, that feeling coming from knowing that someone cared enough to be angry on her behalf. Who had listened to her innermost fear and dismissed its likelihood as nothing other than the result of manipulation and abuse. Who'd said he didn't believe a word of it. Who'd also said she was a great kisser...

And...if the way he'd been looking at her only moments ago was anything to go by, he hadn't been put off by anything she'd told him. He looked as if he wanted to kiss her all over again.

And, heaven help her, but Tilly wanted him to.

Not just yet, though. She wanted to savour this feeling of safety and let it embed itself so it couldn't be lost again. Along with believing that what Harry had implied was correct and there wasn't anything wrong with her sexuality—because, if that was really true, it could change everything.

Possibly her whole life…

CHAPTER EIGHT

IT WAS THE sound of laughter that woke Tilly the next morning.

Male laughter.

Sunlight was streaming through the curtains in what had always been her own room in this wonderful old, rambling house. In the same moment that Tilly realised it was Christmas Eve, she also realised she'd slept in. For someone who was always awake at the crack of dawn, seven-thirty felt like half the morning had been wasted but she felt too good to beat herself up over it. She had, in fact, had a better sleep than she could remember having in…well…possibly her entire adult life.

She hadn't even had any dreams, she thought, as she pulled on a pair of cut-off jeans and a tee shirt after a quick visit to the bathroom. Old clothes, because her brain was waking up properly now and she remembered that they hadn't been able to cut down that baby pine tree her father wanted for the living room. It had been too late by the time she and Harry had got home last night and Tilly had been both physically and emotionally exhausted.

She could hear another shout of laughter as she brushed her hair. Harry's laughter. Suddenly, it was more than Tilly's brain that had woken up. Her body was coming back to the land of the living with surprising enthusiasm. She could feel an echo of that heat she'd felt with Harry's touch when he'd done that bit of play-acting about having fallen in love with her at first sight and it was merging with how she'd felt in the wake of that kiss yesterday—being so hyperaware of every one of her senses—still able to taste him on her tongue, even. But there was a new element to the mix of memories and awareness.

That feeling of safety.

Of hope, perhaps?

Definitely happiness, anyway. Tilly didn't bother taking the time to find shoes or scrape her hair back into the usual tight braid she wore. She could feel her own laughter on the tip of her tongue as she walked into the living room, despite not knowing what was going on.

'What's so funny?' she asked.

Both men looked up and the expressions on their faces made Tilly stop in her tracks. Her father's face was softening with pleasure at seeing her, the crinkles around his eyes and the tenderness of his smile made it almost look as if he was about to shed a tear. It was a look of pure love.

What made Tilly's heart skip a beat was that there was something in the expression on Harry's face that was oddly similar. Apart from a spark of something that *couldn't* have been more different—an appreciation of what was being seen that not only ignited that heat again instantly but threw a significant amount of new fuel on the blaze. She had to look away before she melted into a puddle.

'Oh…you've got a tree already.'

'Your man was up early,' Jim told her. 'He not only helped me get washed and dressed, he went and found the trees and sent me photos so I could choose the perfect one. We were just waiting for you to get up before he cooks breakfast.' He winked at Tilly. 'You've found a keeper this time, love.'

Tilly sucked in a breath. How awful would it be if her father realised that she didn't have any hold on Harry whatsoever so there was no chance of 'keeping' him? He wasn't even planning on staying in the same country as her for much longer. On the plus side, however, at least she didn't have to worry about her father discovering the truth himself, especially having witnessed that kiss last night.

'I wanted to help choose the tree.' She knew she sounded a bit grumpy. She was also staring at the tree propped up in a red bucket, as if she was trying to find fault with a task that had been completed without her involvement. There were strings of lights draped around it and a few decorations had been hung.

'You needed your sleep, sweetheart.' Harry was delving into a cardboard box. 'Oh, my...' He was laughing again. 'It's a leprechaun, so it is.'

Tilly was still staring at the tree as she recognised the decorations already on the tree. The reindeer that looked more like a corgi with very strange ears. The angel that could have been an anaemic bat. 'Oh, no... how could you, Dad? I thought I threw those dreadful things out twenty years ago.'

'I rescued the box from the rubbish bin.' Jim sounded satisfied. 'You made them and they're family treasures. And I do believe that's an elf, not a leprechaun,' he told Harry. 'Although, if it makes you feel at home, lad, there's not that much difference, is there?'

The small figure made out of baked modelling clay had long, spidery green legs and arms and an oversized red hat with a pompom. This was about as embarrassing as having her baby photos displayed. Except, as Harry got to his feet and carried the elf to the tree, he gave her one of those smiles. The kind that was probably responsible for legions of women falling in love with him without any encouragement, but this time it didn't make her feel the slightest resentment.

It made her smile straight back.

And it made her realise that, after last night, she had stepped into the same space all those other women had visited, only to leave with broken hearts. Luckily for Tilly, she knew that any visit she might be making into Harry Doyle's fan club was a very temporary thing and, even if there was something real creeping into the game they were supposed to be playing—on her side, anyway—it was only for a day or two, so it couldn't do any real harm, surely? If anything, it would only make it more convincing when she broke the news to her father that a real relationship had come to an end, with her and Harry going their separate ways.

Harry looped the elf's string around the tip of a branch. 'Brilliant idea to put the string in the middle of his back,' he said. 'Makes him look like he's flying. Wait... I know who this is... He's Super-Elf, isn't he?'

Tilly shook her head, but she was laughing along with both the men and it was suddenly easy to push any misgivings about her feelings for Harry aside. 'I'll get breakfast started,' she said. 'Bacon and eggs?'

'Sounds great,' Jim said. 'I'd kill for a cup of tea too.'

'How's that ankle feeling this morning? Have you had some painkillers?' Tilly went towards her father. 'I should check the swelling in your toes. And your capillary refill.'

'Already done,' Harry said. 'And I'm happy. As long as he's careful to keep his weight off that foot, I think he's well on the road to making a good recovery. Speaking of which—' Harry headed back to the stack of boxes '—we just got a call from the surgeon who took those spikes out of Jase's arm.'

Flashes of the dramatic rescue of the young farmer replayed themselves in Tilly's mind, but the overarching memory was that Harry had been by her side. Keeping her safe as she'd tried to keep Jason's arm safe.

'Is he okay? Has he had surgery yet?'

'He was in Theatre within an hour of the helicopter landing, after they got all the imaging they needed to see whether any major vessels or nerves were involved. He got very lucky—the worst damage was a cracked ulnar, which should heal very quickly.'

'Jase's dad drove his wife, Sandra, up to Dunedin while his mum looked after the kids,' Jim added. 'He got out of surgery about three a.m., but apparently he's well enough this morning for them to agree to discharging him into our care. I said we'd keep a close eye on him and make sure he's taking his antibiotics. He should be back in time to catch the village barbecue and carol singing this evening. Which reminds me, Harry…we need to get that Santa suit out and make sure it fits you. I think it's out in the barn somewhere. Let's hope the mice haven't got into the box. Tilly'll find it, won't you, sweetheart?'

'After breakfast,' she said. 'It was already

on my list. Along with getting that tree decorated—with some proper ornaments. And I want to check on Maggie and then get into Queenstown for a spot of power shopping or there won't be very much under the tree. Then we'll need time to get Harry into his Santa outfit before we head into the village. What time does it all start?'

'Father Christmas needs to be on his throne by five o'clock,' Jim said. 'It takes at least an hour for the photos and chats and there's the games for the kids and then the barbecue. I used to sneak into Sally's house next door to take the suit off while that was happening, and that way I could go into the church for the carol singing at seven o'clock.'

'Is there a rule that Father Christmas doesn't go to church?' Harry sounded curious.

Tilly nodded. 'Church is about the real Christmas story. There's a nativity scene, and old Mrs Baker plays the electric organ for the carols, and everybody gets to hold candles.'

'And I get to go as me,' Jim said. 'It helps keep the secret about who Santa is.' He sighed heavily. 'I look forward to this every year. I wonder if I could persuade Lizzie to take me if we can fit the wheelchair into her car.'

'Lizzie? The nurse who was looking after you yesterday?'

'That's her. She's coming out this morning to make sure I'm behaving myself. And she's on her own since her husband died a few years ago, so she might like some company on Christmas Eve.'

'Oh?' Tilly's eyebrows rose. 'Is there something I should know about going on here?'

'She's a friend,' Jim said. 'That's all.' He leaned back against the pillows on the end of the couch. 'She'll be happy to help me do the tree if she's got the time, but I won't be short on help today. I've been getting calls from all over the district. News sure gets around here fast. Who needs social media when you've got a country town?'

'That's so true,' Tilly murmured.

It was no surprise that she found herself meeting Harry's gaze when she glanced in his direction. He knew how she felt about the lack of privacy in country towns. He was also reminding her that nobody was going to hear anything about Tilly's past from him.

'You can trust me, Tilly. You know that...'

'So you don't have to worry about me being on my own today,' Jim continued, seemingly oblivious to the silent communication going on in front of him. 'You'll be able to take your time and show your man why Queenstown is so famous all over the world.'

Her man.

He was Tilly's man.

It should have been disturbing to know that he was successfully deceiving a man as nice as Jim Dawson, but instead Harry found he was having no problem with the assumption at all.

He *was* Tilly's man. At least until the day after tomorrow, when he had his return flight booked. More importantly, he *wanted* to be Tilly's man—in every sense—even if it was only going to be for a blink of time. He wanted to give her the gift of being able to believe in herself and, if she would let him, he wanted to give her the confidence to embrace her sexuality and stop putting up barriers to a future that could include a partner and maybe even children.

And it felt as if they'd both taken the first step in the right direction last night at the lake. Tilly was wearing shorts this morning, that showed off those long, slim legs. Not only that, she hadn't scraped her hair back in that severe style. It was falling in long, loose waves right down her back and, like her mother in that old photo, she was looking impossibly gorgeous.

Even better, when he'd watched her walk into the living room this morning, he could see *and* feel the difference in the way Tilly was moving in her own skin—more freely, as if an outer shell was much less of a filter to what others could see. She looked…more relaxed. Happier, even?

Whatever. Harry had felt an unspoken but surprisingly strong bond with Jim Dawson in that moment, as they'd both watched her come into the room. For very different reasons, maybe, they both felt proud of her, didn't they? The world, for both of them, had just become a little brighter thanks to Tilly's presence. Happiness was contagious, wasn't it? And it could be given and received at exactly the same time, which only made it bigger.

Better.

They were all at ease with each other enough for banter and laughter to be only a breath away. Soft poached eggs on the toast made from yesterday's sourdough loaf, along with crisp bacon and grilled home-grown tomatoes tasted better than any breakfast Harry had ever had and he blamed Tilly's cooking, a little later, for how tight the Santa suit was when he had to squash the pillow in to do up the wide black belt.

'It's perfect,' Tilly told him. 'You've just got the wig and hat, and the beard, to go on. Oh…and the glasses, of course.' She held out the round gold-rimmed spectacles.

'I'll melt,' Harry warned. 'Have you any idea how hot this outfit is?'

Jim laughed. 'They'll find a shady spot for you. And a cold beer when no one's looking. It's all in a good cause, lad. You'll be amazed what you'll find out about Craig's Gully. Hope you're good at keeping secrets.'

Harry let himself catch Tilly's gaze again. He'd already done his best, this morning, to reassure her that he would never betray her trust, but it was good to be able to say it aloud.

'Keeping secrets is one of my superpowers,' he told Jim. 'Even the torture of being cooked alive in a Santa suit won't drag them out of me.'

* * *

He collected another secret or two after as he and Tilly enjoyed a late lunch at one of the many appealing eateries in the wharf-side area by Queenstown's Lake Wakatipu, in the heart of a crowded shopping district that offered everything from local crafts to designer fashion. Sheltered from the sun by big umbrellas, they ate crayfish salad and watched people bustling past doing their last-minute Christmas shopping.

'Do you think Maggie was being honest when she said she was feeling good today?' Harry was frowning. 'You know her a lot better than I do.'

'I think she was.' Tilly nodded. 'When you were taking the kit back out to the car she told me not to worry because she wasn't going to die this year. She said there was no way she was going to spoil the memory of Christmas Day for any of her grandies.'

'I love Maggie,' Harry said. 'I'd love to have had a grandma like her.'

'Me too.' Tilly smiled. 'But how lucky was I to have her as a surrogate mum when I needed one.'

Perhaps they were both thinking about their mothers as they ate in silence for a while. Harry felt the need to lighten the mood and a glance at the lake, where people were water-skiing in the distance and kayaking closer to shore, made it easy to change the subject.

'There's so much to do here, isn't there?' he commented. 'One of those travel shops we passed had a window full of the stuff you can do around here, and I was having a look while you were choosing that bunch of flowers. You can do four-wheel drive excursions up the Skippers Canyon, Lord of the Rings tours, jet boat adventures. And isn't this where bungee jumping got invented?'

'It really started on a Pacific Island and then got copied by some English guys who were into dangerous hobbies, but this was certainly where it became a thing.'

Harry was still scanning the lake. 'What's the big boat coming in? It looks like a steamship.'

'It is. It's our iconic *TSS Earnslaw*, which I believe is the only remaining coal-fired steamship that takes passengers in the southern hemisphere. I remember my first cruise when I was about four and I thought it was the most exciting thing ever.' Tilly bit her lip. 'Is this when I should confess I'm a total wimp and I've never done the jet boats in the rapids or gone up the Skippers and I have no desire at all to do a bungee jump?'

Harry pulled in a breath, ready to tell Tilly that the last thing in the world he would ever call her was a wimp. That he knew exactly how much courage it had taken to keep her dreadful secret and not only face life but to succeed in everything she'd chosen to do.

He wanted to tell her that, no matter what, he admired her immensely. And that, even if he didn't really have any right to be, he was enormously proud of her. But the opportunity to say anything vanished before the words had gathered coherently because Tilly jumped to her feet.

'On second thoughts, we don't have time for confessions. And I'm sure you've heard enough of mine, anyway.' Tilly wrinkled her nose as she turned away. 'Why don't you stay here and enjoy the view while I finish up getting the boring bits and pieces like wrapping paper and ribbons. I know Dad's favourite shop too, and I'll pop in to get him a new shirt. Something he might not choose for himself.'

'Like a pink one?'

'Yeah…' Tilly grinned. 'Perfect. I'll say it's from both of us.'

'He might hate it.'

'Don't worry, you'll never even know if he doesn't wear it. You'll be on the other side of the world by then.' Tilly was making it sound like a good thing that he'd be so far away. 'We'll have to head back in an hour at the latest, so we've got time to turn you into Father Christmas.'

'I'll go for a wander myself,' Harry said. 'Meet you back where we parked?'

'Good idea. Hey…find yourself some swimming shorts. The forecast is good for tomorrow, and we'll have plenty of time to go for a swim.'

Harry did find himself some shorts he could swim in. He bought a box of craft beer and had it gift-wrapped for Jim, but then a window display in an artisan's workshop caught his eye and he knew exactly what he'd been hoping to find.

Something that would remind Tilly of this blip of time in her life.

That would remind her of him…

She'd done her best to forget about it.

She'd kept herself busy ever since she'd

woken up this morning, but it didn't seem to be helping.

Matilda Dawson wanted Harry to kiss her again and the wanting had been getting stronger and stronger all day. It had kicked into action when he'd given her that look—the one that told her what she already knew—that there was no doubt at all that she could trust him.

The wanting had gone up several notches as he'd kept her laughing over breakfast and she had hoped that the privacy of the old stone-built barn when they went to find the Father Christmas costume might have been enough for the desire to become contagious, but there was no hint that Harry was even thinking about it.

Why would he? Tilly thought. He'd only kissed her last night because they were being watched by her father and it was like producing an ace from his sleeve in the game they were playing.

So maybe we should give him something more interesting to see...?

He'd held her so close last night, beside the lake, but maybe she'd imagined that he ended up looking at her as if he was thinking of kissing her again? Why would he when she'd just finished telling him about the trauma of having been forced to have sex? Maybe all that had been in that look was what she had felt in their closeness. That understanding and tenderness on his part. That feeling of safety on Tilly's part that had unlocked something deep inside that she'd thought she'd lost for ever—the ability to trust a man she didn't know, along with a physical yearning that had clearly distilled into something so much stronger for having been ignored for so many years.

She couldn't initiate something herself, though, in the barn or anywhere else for that matter. Not after the way she had involuntarily reacted to Harry's kiss last night. What if he didn't actually want to kiss her again? And, even if he did, what if she had a panic attack or something in response to anything more than simply a kiss? Even if there was only a limited time that she would be working with Harry before he went home to Ireland, the fact that he knew about something so intimate—so *humiliating*—about her would make everything so much worse.

So…it had to be Harry's choice if or when anything else was going to happen between them. If that turned out to be nothing or never, Tilly still had something that she was always going to be very thankful for. The gratitude made her invent a reason to escape from Harry during their shopping trip to Queenstown. She wanted to find a gift that was special enough to make him realise that he'd given her much more of a gift than giving her father a happy Christmas believing that his daughter had found true love.

Harry had given her the gift of being able to believe that he was right. That there was nothing wrong with her and that she didn't deserve the horrible label of being frigid that she'd allowed herself to believe. Because nobody who had an aversion to sex could feel this level of desire. Or this need for something Tilly had believed she could never want again and…and it was making her feel alive.

Not the kind of alive that had become almost an addiction in the last ten years—with that adrenaline rush of facing an intense situation when someone's life was in danger and your heart was racing and every sense was heightened. The kind of rush that was the reason why she loved working in the emergency department so much and could never have imagined wanting the quieter working life of a rural GP.

But this kind of alive could also make your heart speed up, couldn't it? It could heighten every sense like taste and touch and make even the colours around you and the warmth of the sunshine on your skin seem more intense. Maybe the difference was the destination. The aftermath of fighting for someone's life could leave you feeling either victorious or defeated but it was also a state of being that was hard to unwind from.

The destination that *this* kind of being alive could take you to was the complete opposite.

Peace.

Contentment.

The feeling of coming home after a long day's work, where you could take a deep breath and simply *be*…

Like the way she'd felt in Harry's arms last night, when the tears had gone and her fear had been washed away with them.

The feeling of home but with the bonus of not being there alone.

With that thought humming in the back of her mind, it turned out to be very easy to choose the gift she was searching for.

It had everything. It would remind Harry of his time in New Zealand. It had a meaning that captured the essence of what he had given her with the promise of potentially a new life. It was something he could keep close so he would never forget, but he could also keep it private. As private as the secret he was keeping on her behalf.

Best of all, he would be able to see it. And touch it. And it would remind him of her.

CHAPTER NINE

IT WAS STARTING to feel a lot more like Christmas when Tilly and Harry arrived back at the old family villa after their shopping expedition.

Suddenly, there was too much to do. They needed to change clothes and head into the township for the Christmas gathering in Craig's Gully, but there were parcels and bags to be unpacked from the Jeep and hidden carefully so that surprises didn't get spoilt if they ran out of time to wrap gifts. There was Christmas music playing and the living room was a bombsite, with emptied boxes and packing materials scattered everywhere but also with a magnificently decorated tree, its lights already twinkling and parcels underneath.

Lizzie had been there helping Jim Dawson

with the decorations for hours and she wasn't leaving any time soon, apparently.

'I've told him he can't go to the barbecue,' she told Tilly, 'and now I'll have to stay long enough to make sure he doesn't try to persuade anyone else to take him out gallivanting around the countryside.'

'It smells like you're already cooking dinner. Or have you been baking?'

'People have been coming by. Bringing casseroles and mince pies and gingerbread and all sorts of other things to go under the tree. I think it's a bit of a shock that their beloved local doctor could have killed himself falling off the roof.'

Tilly didn't need to see that hint of a smile on Harry's face as he slid a quick glance in her direction to remember what he'd said about being a country GP and being significant in the lives of so many people. That a whole community could become like a family. Seeing the love and support that was coming out for her father did make it seem like a balance to the side of a close-knit community that Tilly couldn't handle—the gossip and judgement that came from everybody knowing too much about everybody else.

She was still thinking about it when she

was getting changed into a summer dress, having hidden her parcels in the back of her wardrobe. She might have been an only child but the bond she had with her father was unbreakable. She knew that kind of bond was the same but with more strands to it in bigger families and she'd seen the support of family groups gathering in the emergency department over many years now.

There was a special glue in those bonds that came, at least in part, from knowing everything. You celebrated the good stuff but you still accepted people despite any not so good stuff and that was the kind of acceptance that built and strengthened those bonds. It had to be a diluted form of that glue that brought unrelated people in communities together. And a not so diluted form that created real friendships.

Like the friendship that seemed to be forming between herself and Harry? He knew about her bad stuff but he not only accepted her, he seemed to like her more. To care more.

Tilly paused for a moment after pulling sandals onto her bare feet.

It felt good, this bond that was forming with Harry.

So good that, like seeing the outpouring of concern from the community for her father, it made Tilly wonder if she'd made a mistake by allowing herself to become so distant. Why had she spent so much of her life trying to be so independent, anyway? To prove that she didn't desperately miss her mother when she wasn't around so that people wouldn't feel sorry for her? Because she adored her father and didn't want him to feel any worse when he was already stressed, trying to cover all parental duties when he was missing his beloved wife and he still had to respond to all the needs of a community that depended on him? Whatever the reason had been, Tilly had learned as a child that she could cope on her own and had believed it had stood her in good stead when it had felt as if her life was falling apart as an adult. Had it, instead, been the foundation for barriers she'd strengthened ever since?

Perhaps it was because it was Christmas that was making her so aware of the concept of family. Maybe it was because of her father's accident. Or it could be that something else was the catalyst for what was making Tilly's heart feel as if it had broken out of some kind of cage and was filling up more than it had ever been able to do before. Making her yearn for things she had believed she would never be able to have.

It seemed quite likely that that something else was Harry Doyle...

Tilly's soft cotton, floaty dress was a complete contrast to Harry, who was resplendent in the full Father Christmas attire designed for a northern hemisphere Christmas as she drove him into Craig's Gully township late that afternoon.

The grass square with a war memorial in its centre was a hive of activity.

There were old oak trees around the edges of the grass square, which provided some welcome shade.

'There's your throne.' Tilly pointed to an oversized chair, covered in red velvet, under one of the trees. A Christmas tree covered in shiny baubles was on one side of the ornate throne and two small ponies with reindeer antlers on their heads and strands of tinsel tied into shaggy manes and tails were tethered on the other side beside a large bucket of water.

'They look like the ponies Maggie's grandchildren were riding yesterday,' Tilly said.

'Thank goodness they're in the shade. Along with my throne.' Harry pushed the white curls of his wig off his forehead. 'I knew it was crazy to have Christmas in the middle of summer. I've only got my togs on underneath this outfit but I'm already cooking. The coat is sticking to my back, and you have no idea how itchy this beard is.'

Tilly could only offer him a sympathetic smile. One that melted into something even softer as she noticed that his ears were showing through the curls beneath a hat that was a size too small.

'You're a hero for doing this, Harry,' she said. 'My dad thinks you're the best thing since sliced bread and that I'm the luckiest girl in the world.'

She had to look away from Harry now. Away from those adorable ears and those captivating blue eyes. She didn't want him to see anything in her face that might make him wonder if this pretence might be getting a bit out of hand. To see something that might make him feel sorry for her when they stepped back into reality the day after tomorrow? The way he'd felt about having to disappoint that young nurse, Charlotte?

Thank goodness she could make it sound

as if she was simply going along with how well Harry's acting gig was going in public.

'Look…you've got more members of your fan club already.'

A small queue was forming in the shade on the Christmas tree side of the throne. A young mother with a toddler in her arms, another pushing a pram and several older children who were unaccompanied. Their parents were no doubt amongst the adults who were firing up the barbecue grills, setting food out on trestle tables in another shady spot and organising games for the children. Someone's father was setting up a camera to record the annual tradition of sitting beside Father Christmas and spilling their most secret wishes.

'I remember coming here,' she told Harry. 'And even though I knew it was my dad being Santa, I still loved it. When I got older I couldn't understand why people did this on a day when they would already be so busy, the day before Christmas, but… I think I get it now. Tomorrow is plenty of time for all the smaller families to be together. This is celebrating that big family you were talking about.'

She waved a hand at the scene around

them. Someone was handing out ice creams from a half wine barrel full of ice and another barrel had cold drinks for the adults. 'You were right when you pointed out that there's a positive side to everyone knowing your business. I think I'm only just realising how much I've missed it.'

Was it because those barriers she'd probably started building way back when she was just a kid, missing her mum, and had made impenetrable after the trauma of the assault, were starting to crumble? Because she felt different since last night?

Because of Harry...?

That internal melty feeling was threatening to bring tears to her eyes. The need to give something back to Harry suddenly seemed of the utmost importance because... good grief...this felt like a whole lot more than gratitude for anything he'd done for her.

It felt a lot like love...

She caught his gaze. 'I'm beginning to think being a GP in Craig's Gully might not be such a bad thing,' she said quietly. 'And I think I get why you feel you need to go back home to Ireland. I really hope you find what you're looking for there because...you deserve to be happy, Harry.'

Tilly also wanted to tell him how special he really was. How very glad she was that he'd offered to come home and share Christmas with her. She could have even told him that she loved him in that moment—in a light-hearted kind of way that a friend could say it so it wouldn't lead to any awkwardness later—but the arrival of Father Christmas had been spotted and excited children were jumping up and down.

'Santa! Santa! Santa!'

'Good luck,' was all she had the chance to say in the end. 'I'll come and save you from heatstroke later.'

If he hadn't been quietly cooking inside the Santa suit, this would have been quite fun. Harry had never been into dressing-up so it was a novelty to be disguised so well that, even if people knew him, he couldn't be recognised. Tilly was the only person here who knew who was inside the suit and he liked that it was a secret just between them. He sat on the throne and had small children sitting on his knee, babies in his arms, older children sitting on cushions beside him and even dogs lying at his feet as photographs were taken and secrets were whispered. He heard about the toys and games and electronic devices that children were hoping would arrive overnight.

Tilly turned up with an icy cold beer in a paper cup.

'Ho-ho-ho!' Harry said. 'You're a good girl, Matilda.'

'The queue's getting shorter,' she told him. 'Hang in there. Can you see the little girl in the pink tutu?'

Harry peered over the top of the gold-rimmed spectacles. 'Yes.'

'That's Ava. Jase's daughter?'

'Ah…' Harry finished his drink and handed Tilly the empty cup. 'Do you think he remembers the promise I made to find out what she wants for Christmas?'

'I know he does. He just asked me to remind you.'

Tilly pointed to where picnic rugs and chairs were being set up near the tables and, sure enough, Jase was sitting on one of the chairs, his arm in a sling and a smile on his face.

When it was Ava's turn to whisper her secret, Harry found himself holding his breath, but the little girl was suddenly shy.

'What is it that you'd like Father Christmas to bring you, pet?'

'I forget...'

'Have a think about it while we smile for our photo. Is that your mummy there? With your baby brother?'

'Yes. My daddy's got a sore arm.'

'I know. But it's going to get all better soon. Can you see my reindeer?'

'They're not reindeer,' Ava giggled. 'They're ponies.'

Harry lowered his voice. 'Do you like ponies, Ava?'

'I love ponies,' she whispered back.

'Is that what you'd really like for Christmas?'

Ava nodded and Harry patted her head. 'I'll see what I can do.' He raised his voice to a cheerful boom. 'Merry Christmas. Ho-ho-ho...'

Right at the end of the queue were the twins he recognised as Maggie's grandchildren. They were both wearing red headbands with Christmas decorations on them.

'Which one of you is Sammy and which one is George?' he asked.

'I'm George.' The girl had three tiny angels on her headband. 'And he's Sammy.'

Sammy had a Christmas tree made of green felt on his headband. It was decorated with tiny golden balls and bows made of silver tinsel.

'How do you know our names?' Sammy sounded suspicious.

'I'm Father Christmas. I know everything.'

'You're not the real Father Christmas. He's at the North Pole and he doesn't get here till tomorrow.'

'Okay…you got me.' Harry was too hot and tired to argue. 'I'm one of his helpers.'

'Where's the real one?'

'He's busy wrapping presents. And loading up his sleigh. He comes to New Zealand first, did you know that?'

'Which way does he come?'

'From the north.'

'Which way's that?'

'Um…' Harry wasn't sure, so he waved vaguely at the hills. 'Up there. He'll come over the top of those hills later tonight so you'd better tell me what it is you're hoping for most of all so I can get a message to him.'

'We already wrote him a letter,' George told him.

'That's good.' Harry nodded. 'But you could tell me too.'

'We both want the same thing.' Sammy still sounded suspicious. 'If you know our names you should know about that too. Unless the letter didn't get there…'

George tugged on his sleeve. 'I'll tell you,' she whispered. She knelt up on her cushion and put her mouth so close to his ear that it tickled. He could hear her gulp of breath that advertised how important this was. 'We want Nana to get better.'

Oh…

Harry closed his eyes in a long blink as he pulled in a breath.

'I know what she said,' Sammy growled into the silence. 'So…?'

Harry looked down at the small boy, still lost for words.

'So…can you do that?' Sammy demanded.

'I'm so sorry that your nana's sick,' Harry said carefully. 'But I know that it's very special for her to be able to have this Christmas with you.'

'So you're not going to make her better.' Sammy glared at Harry as he slid off his cushion. 'You can't, anyway, because you're not the real Father Christmas. Come on, George.'

But George sat there for a moment longer,

gazing up at Harry with tears about to spill from her eyes.

Harry bent his head and spoke softly. 'Sometimes, getting better can be about when things stop hurting,' he said.

George nodded slowly. 'Like when my foot stopped hurting,' she said, 'After Geronimo stood on it.'

'Is Geronimo your pony? I mean your reindeer?'

'No, he's Sammy's pony. My pony is called Bilbo and he's too kind to step on anybody's toes.' She was smiling as she climbed off the throne. 'I need to go and find Sammy,' she said. 'And my mum. She said we could have an ice cream next and maybe that will make Sammy feel not quite so sad.'

Harry took off his spectacles as he watched her go after her brother. He was using the sleeve of his jacket to wipe his eyes as Tilly appeared from nowhere.

Her brow furrowed as she looked up at him. 'Are you okay?'

'I don't think I've ever been this hot in my entire life,' Harry told her. 'I might actually have hyperthermia.' He let his breath out in a sigh. 'And I just had Maggie's grandchildren tell me that the only thing they want for Christmas is for their nana to get better.'

'Oh…' Tilly's eyes seemed to get bigger and darker. She looked over her shoulder at the crowd of people sharing food and laughter as children played around them. And then she looked back at Harry and he knew that she knew being part of that group was the last thing he wanted right now.

She held out her hand.

'Come with me,' she said. 'I know exactly where you need to be.'

The lake was deserted.

Tilly knew it would be, because everybody who might have been there was at the barbecue in the town square, so this was not only private, she'd known it would provide exactly the kind of serenity that Harry badly needed.

She needed a bit of it herself, to be honest. Harry had told her, word for word, about his conversation with Sammy and George and his suggestion that Maggie being free of her pain was a form of 'getting better' had squeezed her heart enough to bring tears to her eyes.

He was going to make the best father ever,

she thought as she brought the Jeep to a halt. And the woman he chose to be the mother of those six children was yet to discover how lucky she was.

The lake was as still as a mill pond. The scorching heat of the sun was softening as the long summer twilight began, but the stones of the beach had soaked up the warmth enough to make the clear, cool water of this small lake even more inviting.

Harry had removed the big black belt and unzipped the jacket of his suit, throwing the pillow into the back of the Jeep as Tilly had driven him here. He had also discarded the hat, wig, beard and spectacles and kicked off the black boots, but he still looked…almost shell-shocked.

'Why don't you get the rest of your kit off?' she suggested as soon as they were standing on the beach.

'What?'

'You've said you put your swimming shorts on underneath, didn't you?'

'Yes, but…'

'It's going to be the fastest way for you to cool off. I can pretty much guarantee we've got this place to ourselves for a while, so you could go skinny-dipping if you prefer. I won't look...'

Tilly tried to find a smile but found her lips were strangely wobbly as she remembered what Harry had said only yesterday about having to go swimming naked because he hadn't brought his togs with him. It felt a lot longer ago than yesterday. A lifetime ago, in some ways...because this wasn't stirring feelings that were going to make her unbearably nervous. Tilly couldn't feel even a hint of that kind of fear and the relief was as overwhelming as whatever emotions Sammy and George had stirred in Harry.

Standing there with his sweat-dampened curls, bare feet, the pants of his suit rolled up to his calves and the red and white jacket open so that his bare chest was visible was making Harry Doyle the sexiest Santa Claus imaginable but, also strangely, Tilly wasn't feeling any shafts of that heat that she was learning could be triggered by physical desire. She wasn't even thinking about wanting Harry to kiss her again.

This was something deeper. Emotional rather than physical. This was about things that were going to be lost, like the grief that Maggie's grandchildren were going to have to experience soon. It was about things that had already been lost, like both their own mothers. Like Tilly's ability to trust. Or take risks. And about whatever it was that had been keeping Harry from finding what he was searching for. There was love in that mix too. The love that Harry had to give. Her gratitude—and love—for what he'd already given her.

This was about life, Tilly realised. As huge and complicated and wonderful and sad as it all was and how much it mattered to find a connection with another human who could be there when it was all a bit too much.

Harry hadn't moved. He was staring at Tilly as though he was seeing her for the first time, but she couldn't blame him. Just a day or so ago he wouldn't have believed that the 'Ice Queen' would be suggesting a skinny-dip. She wouldn't have believed it herself.

Not that she was going to go quite that far. Tilly was wearing a perfectly respectable bra and panties under her dress.

'Last one in's a rotten egg,' she announced, reaching for the hem of her dress so she could pull it off over her head.

The stones hurt her feet and the water was cold enough to make her squeak, so Tilly had to keep going until it was deep enough to dive and then swam as hard as she could. By the time she surfaced her body was adjusting to the temperature of the water. She used her legs and arms to keep her head above water, waiting for that delicious moment when it would start to feel like cool silk rippling around her body, and she scanned the lake around her to see where Harry was.

There was no sign of him.

She could see the heap of red and white fabric on the beach, so he'd stripped off, but if he'd followed her into the lake he hadn't left so much as a ripple. A beat of alarm made Tilly's breath catch in her throat. Had Harry been even more overheated than she'd realised? Had the sudden immersion in cold water given him cramps or a cardiac arrhythmia? Had he sunk without a trace and was drowning?

The squeak Tilly had made on entering the water was nothing to the squeal as she felt her ankle being gripped and tugged. Her head went underwater but she was released instantly and she came up spluttering—with laughter. The best she could manage in return was to scoop water in her hand and aim it for Harry's face. The water fight that ensued lasted for a good ten minutes and left them both exhausted and breathless, from treading water and laughing so hard. By tacit agreement, when they found themselves in water at neck level when their feet could touch the stone bed of the lake, a truce was called and they stayed still as the ripples subsided and the echoes of their laughter vanished into the fading light.

It was Tilly who broke the silence. 'Feeling better?'

Harry grinned at her. 'So much better.'

'Want to get out?'

Harry shook his head. 'I think I might want to stay here for ever.'

Tilly smiled. 'For ever is quite a long time, you know.'

'I might change my mind in a minute or two. It *is* getting colder.'

'I think I'm getting goosebumps.'

She felt Harry's finger brush her arm under the water. 'You are. Okay…it's time to get out.'

Except neither of them made any movement other than the gentle rocking that meant they could keep their balance in the water and, although the water was crystal clear, the ripples were enough to blur the image of their bodies so the only part of Harry that Tilly was aware of was his face. He had wet hair plastered to his head and she could even see droplets of water in the tangle of his eyelashes, but it was those astonishing blue eyes that captured her. No. It was the way he was looking at her.

There was no one watching them. No one to appreciate any performance intended to convince them that Harry was head over heels in love with her, but that was how this gaze was making Tilly feel. She had no idea whether her foot slipped on the pebbles beneath them, or whether there was some mysterious current in the lake that made it happen, but it felt as if she simply floated even closer to Harry and it was instinctive to catch her balance by reaching out to touch the bare skin of his shoulders. The warmth of his arms coming around her should have counteracted the goosebumps caused by the cold water but, in fact, she could feel them become more pronounced when she lifted her face and felt the touch of Harry's lips against hers.

It was when she felt the soft, silky touch of his tongue against hers that she was aware of a warmth through her entire body that no chilly lake water could possibly compete with. A warmth that made it impossible for Tilly to freeze, in any sense, and there was only one thing she wanted to do.

Kiss Harry back.

And to stay here for ever.

They'd been in the water for too long.

As welcome as the cooling effect had been after hours of sweltering in that Santa suit, when he felt Tilly beginning to shiver in his arms Harry knew it was time to get out.

Which meant it was time to stop kissing her as well. But maybe that was a good thing because he couldn't quite remember whose idea it had been to do it in the first place and he had to be very, very sure that it was something that Tilly wanted as much as he did.

The stones on the beach still held the heat of the sun but Harry draped the jacket of the Santa suit around Tilly's shoulders.

'Have you got a towel in the car?'

'No. Just the bag with your change of clothes. I wasn't planning on swimming.'

'Of course you weren't. You should still be at the barbecue. Do you want to head back?'

'It'll be all over by now. The carol service will be just about finished. Everybody will be heading home so they can get the kids to bed as early as possible.' Tilly smiled. 'They'll probably be up again at about five a.m. when it starts getting light. Another disadvantage of having Christmas in the middle of summer, I guess.'

'I think I'm starting to like it,' Harry said. 'There's something about this place. Something that feels like Christmas even when it shouldn't. It's breaking all the rules.'

'Like roaring fires and mulled wine and lots of snow?'

'Exactly.'

'Did you always get a white Christmas in Dublin?'

'Not at all. It only happens once every few years. I've got a photo of one when I was about eight. I think it was 1995. My mam and I built the best snowman ever, with lumps of coal for his eyes and buttons and proper forked branches so that his arms had hands with fingers.'

'No… I don't believe it. Fingers?'

'I've got a photo. I'll prove it to you. I gave him my hat and scarf to wear.'

'I'd like to see that.'

He could hear the smile in Tilly's voice but didn't turn his head to see it.

'Everyone said the most spectacular white Christmas ever in Dublin was in 2010,' he told her. 'There was so much snow and it made everything so much prettier. Even the tenement block Mam was still living in didn't look so bad with all the edges softened and the lights shining.' Harry stared out at the still lake, as if he could see the reflections of his own life in its surface. 'She was already sick with the cancer, but she never told me about it. And that was the last Christmas we ever had together...'

It had to be trickles of water still escaping from his hair that were rolling down his face like tears. Harry didn't cry. He'd learned not to when he'd been about Sammy's age, because it only made the bullying worse. It was time to make someone laugh. Himself as well as Tilly with any luck, if he could think of a good joke.

But then he heard the tiniest sound of a sniff and, when he turned his head, he saw Tilly rubbing her nose. He could see the tears making those dark eyes of hers shimmer in this soft light and the knowledge that she had absorbed his own pain made something shift in his chest. Something that moved enough to give his heart room to expand. Yeah…this felt like Christmas.

Because it felt like family. It felt like love. And wasn't that what Christmas was all about?

Harry reached out to use the pad of his thumb to brush away a tear that escaped, curling his fingers around her jawbone at the same time. Because he wanted to kiss this woman again. And again.

He wanted, very much, to make love to her, if Tilly wanted him to. And if it happened to be on a deserted lake beach as daylight faded, using a Santa suit to cushion the stones, it could well become the most favourite Christmas memory ever.

Tilly knew what he was thinking. He could see his own thoughts reflected in her eyes. He could feel the warmth of her skin as he leaned towards her. And he heard the sharp intake of her breath. Not because of his touch, though. There was another sound they could both hear—the demanding ring of a phone coming from the front seat of the Jeep.

'I'd better get that,' Tilly said, pulling the jacket around her as she scrambled to her feet. 'Nobody would call at this time of night on Christmas Eve if it wasn't something important.'

CHAPTER TEN

THE TENSION IN Tilly's voice cut through the serenity of their surroundings like a knife.

'How long ago? Where's George? Is someone with Maggie?'

Harry was on his feet and pulling clothes from the bag on the back seat well before she finished the call. He knew the people that were being discussed. He knew that, somehow, he was involved.

And Tilly's expression confirmed it.

'Remember what you said to Sammy?' she asked. 'About where the real Father Christmas is?'

'That he was in the North Pole?'

'That he would be coming over the hills later tonight. That was Dad on the phone. He got a call from Doug Grimshaw, who wanted to talk to you about what you'd said. Apparently, George told him that Sammy's gone to find Father Christmas. He wanted George to go with him, but she was scared so he said he'd go by himself, and she wasn't allowed to tell anybody because it was a secret.'

Harry's heart sank like a stone. 'He thinks the "real" Father Christmas can make his wish come true. That I couldn't do it because I was only his helper.'

'And now he's disappeared,' Tilly said. 'They didn't stay for the carol service because they had arranged for someone to video call from the church and the family were going to join in from around Maggie's bed. The twins said they wanted to put the ponies back in the paddock by themselves and take all the tinsel off. That was a while ago now and nobody knows where Sammy is and he took his pony so he could have gone quite a long way already. People are heading up to the Grimshaws' farm to help look for him. If they can't find him before it starts getting dark they'll have to call in Search and Rescue, but there's no guarantee there'll be a full team available on Christmas Eve.'

'This is partly my fault.' Harry said quietly. 'I need to be there. I have to help.'

* * *

When Tilly and Harry went home to get some warmer clothes and suitable footwear for trekking up hills on a high-country sheep station, it was clear that Jim Dawson felt just as strong a need to be there.

'I delivered those twins,' he said gruffly. 'And Maggie was your mum's best friend, Tilly. I'm part of that family. Harry, go and find some woollen jumpers in the chest of drawers in my room and bring one for me as well. Grab some socks while you're at it. I reckon my gumboots will be a perfect fit for you.'

'I'll stay with him,' Lizzie said. 'Have you got some camping chairs? That way, I can at least make sure he's not standing around too much on his crutches.'

'We need torches. And spare batteries. I'll find them,' Tilly said.

'Should we fill some Thermoses with hot water?' Lizzie asked. 'And take some of that baking that's been arriving all day?'

'With any luck they will have found Sammy by the time we get up there,' Tilly said, 'but yeah… I'm sure a cup of tea and a mince pie would still be welcome.'

They were far from the only people to

have thought of what might be needed if a missing child wasn't found in a hurry. A paddock near the gate to the homestead gardens was filling up with utes and four-wheel drive farm vehicles. Even the local fire engine and a police car were parked on the grass. A trestle table that had probably just been packed up recently from the barbecue in the town square was already laden with plates of food people had brought and there was a small platoon of Thermoses to one side. Jim Dawson, propped up on his crutches, took over organising mugs and bottles of milk. Tilly saw him wave a hand at Lizzie, probably dismissing her suggestion that it was time he sat down somewhere and put his foot up.

The paddock could be seen from the homestead further up the hill and Tilly could imagine that Maggie was sitting in her bed, watching what was happening. Feeling sick with worry about her grandson. It felt as if everyone was worried sick as she walked with Harry towards the group of people gathering at another gate that led onto a bare hill beside the driveway. There were people on horseback coming very slowly down the slope and one of them was leading a pony.

'It's Geronimo,' someone said. 'Look, he's still got a bit of that tinsel tied to his tail.'

'But where's Sammy? I can't see him.'

'That pony's limping. He's hurt himself.'

'Probably put his foot in a rabbit hole. They're everywhere up there.'

'Better than a mine shaft.' A man's quiet voice was grim. 'There's plenty of those around in these hills too.'

One of the men on horseback was Doug, and Tilly assumed the man beside him was his older brother, John, the twins' father. They had farm dogs with them and someone following on a quad bike. It was Doug who spoke to the group waiting for them.

'We found Geronimo up past the ridge where there's a patch of beech forest. It's too rocky for the quad bikes past there and dangerous for the horses now that it's getting dark.' He cleared his throat. 'There's no sign of Sam, and if he could hear us calling he's not answering.'

Tilly caught Harry's gaze. That his uncle was using his formal name made this all sound so much more serious. That Sammy wasn't responding to calls when he had to be frightened after falling off his pony was even more worrying. Was he hurt? Unconscious? Harry was wearing a large backpack that was filled with first aid gear from her father's vehicle. Tilly was wearing a smaller one that contained a drug kit and a small oxygen cylinder. They would be ready to deal with whatever they found—if they could find Sammy in time.

'We've been in touch with the police and available mountain search and rescue personnel are being contacted and will be on their way from Queenstown asap. In the meantime, some of us can fan out and start a search on foot. Bruce is over there near the table, and he'll take your details if you want to join the line and he'll make sure you've got a torch and a means of communication. We've got a few two-way radios available, but he'll take your phone numbers and make sure you've got his. Tilly—we're going to put you in charge of anything medical that's needed, is that okay?'

'Of course.'

'Go and see Bruce and he'll make sure you've got a radio.'

'Bruce was our local cop when I was growing up,' Tilly told Harry as they turned away. 'I thought he would have retired long ago.'

And maybe he had but he was here tonight,

along with so many other concerned friends and neighbours, even if they couldn't do anything to help other than being here—like her father. They were here to offer support. To be part of the caring. Tilly had that feeling of her heart filling to overflowing again, but this time she couldn't attribute it to the bond she could feel with Harry or because it was Christmas. This was definitely about family and, more specifically, the kind of family that Harry had reminded her existed in a form large enough to contain an entire community.

It was in that moment that Tilly recognised the deep yearning she had to come home. To live and work in this rugged country, amongst people that she already cared about. That she could trust would care about her.

Doug was off his horse now and loosening the girth of his saddle. Someone was leading Geronimo away.

'At least we know he's in this paddock,' Doug called as people began moving towards where Bruce was stationed. 'But it's a big one. At least ten acres and it gets pretty gnarly further up past the native bush. Don't join the line unless you're a confident tramper. Stay in pairs and please…be careful. We don't want anyone else hurt up there.'

Anyone *else*…

Without thinking, Tilly found herself reaching for Harry's hand as they followed the group. Feeling the squeeze of his fingers curl around hers and, even better, that he didn't let it go added enough extra to whatever was filling her heart to make it ache—as if this addition had jagged edges.

Because, when she came home to this place and these people she loved, she was going to be a world away from Harry and she would never feel his hand holding hers again and Tilly had the disturbing feeling that the ache she could feel in her heart right now might be only the tip of an iceberg she could never have dreamed was even on the horizon. She pulled in a deep breath to steady herself and Harry must have heard it because he turned his head to catch her gaze.

'We'll find him,' he said. 'Because we won't stop until we do.'

Tilly could feel the level of Harry's involvement in this disappearance of a small boy. She could hear his determination to succeed and how imperative it was that they *did* succeed and…and she loved him for caring that much.

She loved him for who he was.

She had fallen in love with Harry Doyle, it was as simple as that.

The consequences of her heart being stolen so unexpectedly would have to wait. For now, Tilly welcomed the rush of warmth that came with acknowledging that love because it brought with it a wash of hope.

They were going to find Sammy.

This would be okay.

It *had* to be okay. Because anything else was unthinkable on the eve of Christmas Day.

The temperature dropped as daylight faded and the shadows of the uneven, rocky ground became a minefield of accidents, like a sprained ankle or a broken wrist, waiting to happen.

That was why Harry was keeping a firm hold of Tilly's hand in one of his, using his other hand to hold the torch and shine light into crevasses between big rocks that could easily hide a small boy who didn't want to be found until *he'd* found Father Christmas.

'Sammy,' he called. '*Sam*-my…'

It sounded like an echo of his own voice coming from the right, above the level that he and Tilly were searching, but it was someone else calling amidst the beams of other torches that flickered amongst the rocks and trees like giant fireflies.

They'd been here for what felt like hours now and Harry could swear they'd been over this exact patch of ground already. Admittedly, the initial search was hit and miss as everybody wanted to be out here searching far and wide as quickly as possible, but it had become more coordinated after the experienced members of a local search and rescue team took command. Quad bikes and a tractor had ferried people and supplies as far as they could so that a base was established for mapping the area into a grid and beginning a methodical search that would cover every square metre. And someone was on their way to the farm with a specialised search dog that had raised everyone's hopes.

'He can't have got far,' the searchers said, when they'd gathered to be reassigned sections of the huge paddock.

'Yeah…it's too steep for anyone to go further up.'

'And don't forget the headband. He's got to be here somewhere.'

The news that the red headband with the Christmas tree attached had been found, thanks to the glitter of the silver tinsel catching a beam of torchlight, had been relayed to the camp at the bottom paddock by the driveway and the searchers had all heard the cheer go up.

Maggie had probably heard that cheer from the house and must have thought that Sammy had been found but that was at least an hour ago now and nothing more had been discovered. Harry's heart felt more and more heavy at the thought of what it must be like in that big, overdecorated room where Maggie's bed was. Did she have George cuddled up beside her and any members of the family who weren't out searching sitting close enough to be able to reach out and touch them both? He hoped so. He liked Maggie. He liked everyone he'd met so far in Craig's Gully and right now he'd give anything to have a chance to talk to Sammy again.

He'd like to tell him that he knew how hard this was but that it would be okay. That, as long as Sammy had the people he loved and who loved him close by, he would be able to get through this. That he was needed. By Maggie. And his twin sister. And his mum and dad and everybody else in that big, loving Grimshaw family.

It could get you through anything, that kind of love.

'I can hear dogs barking,' Tilly said. 'It could be that the farm dogs have spotted a stranger arriving. Maybe that search dog will be able to sniff the headband and take us straight to where Sammy is.'

'It would have been better if the person who found it hadn't picked it up and taken it down the hill. It'll take longer for the dog to pick up the trail.'

Or maybe it wouldn't. The dark shape that appeared from behind them made Harry utter an oath and pull Tilly close, but the German Shepherd took no notice of either of them. He had his nose down and a long rope trailing behind him as he went past. The man on the other end of the rope sounded out of breath as he caught up.

'It's steeper…than it looks…eh?'

His dog was out of sight around a jagged tumble of rock, but the volley of barking was loud enough to make Tilly jump.

'He's found something,' the dog's handler called back. 'Follow me… No…wait…'

Harry pulled Tilly to a stop. He could see the dog, still barking, but it was facing them and there was nothing but grass and tussock to be seen in the space between them as he played his torchlight over the ground.

'Stay there,' the man ordered. 'Something's not quite right.' He had his own torch and he moved forward slowly. 'Good boy... Kobe. What have you found, mate?'

There was a long moment's silence, broken only by an exclamation of disbelief. And then both the dog and man lay down on the ground and they heard him call, 'Sammy? You down there, buddy? Can you hear me?'

The sound of a child's cry in return made Tilly gasp and brought a lump the size of a golf ball into Harry's throat.

'I'm in here... I can't get out...'

'That's what we're here for, buddy. You're going to hear me blowing a whistle now. I'm calling in the troops.'

Tilly met Harry's gaze as he reached for the two-way radio he was carrying. 'And I'm calling Maggie...'

There had to be dozens of people on the Grimshaws' land. Thousands and thousands of sheep scattered over these hills and all sorts of wild animals like rabbits and deer, goats and possums and owls, but it felt as if every living creature was holding its breath.

As if the whole world was focused on this small hole in the ground—an old, abandoned mineshaft that had been dug well over a century ago and had been partly filled in and narrowed by erosion over the decades. It had been just big enough for a small boy to slip inside, dislodging stones and dry earth in his attempts to get out, which only made him fall further but, thankfully, seemed to have prevented any significant injuries.

'My knee's a bit sore,' Sammy told Harry as he questioned him thoroughly to try and do a remote assessment. 'But that might have been from when I fell off Geronimo. I was riding him without his saddle and it made him a bit slippery.'

'It was a very brave thing to do.' Harry was lying on his stomach, shining a torch down into the hole, being careful not to make the edges crumble and rain dirt on the small, hunched figure he could see. Tilly was lying on the other side of the hole.

Sammy's voice wobbled. 'Am I in big trouble?'

'No, darling.' It was Tilly who reassured him. 'I reckon everybody's going to be too happy to get you home to be cross.'

'Can I come out now?'

'Just as soon as we get sorted,' Harry said. 'We've got the people who know how to do stuff like this, so we need to let them make a plan. It could take a wee while. Is it cold down there?'

'Yes…and… I'm a bit scared.'

Harry pulled off the woollen jersey he was wearing. 'I'm going to drop this jumper,' he told Sammy. 'Don't worry—it's soft and cuddly. If you put it on, it'll help keep you warm.'

'What's a jumper?'

'It's a jersey,' Tilly told him. 'Harry comes from Ireland, and they have different names for some things.'

'He sounds like Santa's helper.'

'You know what? They have little people called leprechauns in Ireland and they look a bit like the elves that are Santa's helpers. And do you want to know a secret?'

The big sniff from the bottom of the hole was a sign that Sammy was fighting tears. 'Y-yes…'

Tilly leaned further into the hole. 'Don't tell anybody, but Harry's got ears just like a leprechaun.'

Harry wriggled back and got to his feet as Tilly coached Sammy into putting on the woollen jersey he'd dropped. The group of men who had coils of rope over their shoulders and harnesses dangling from their hands were waiting for his report.

'I don't think he's injured. He might have grazed or bumped his knee but he can move all his limbs, he's not bleeding and he's oriented and alert. But he's cold and tired and scared so I'm not sure how well he'd manage trying to get himself safely into a harness so we could pull him up.'

'He hasn't managed to get his arms into the sleeves of that jersey.' Tilly had joined the group. 'I wouldn't trust his ability to deal with the buckles on a harness.'

'And the shaft is too tight for any of us to get down. We'd just make it collapse further by trying.'

'It's only about five metres at the most.'

'We could dig in from the side,' someone suggested. 'Just a few metres of a channel would be enough. Then someone could lean in and catch his wrists and haul the poor wee blighter out. If he stood up maybe it wouldn't even need to be that deep.'

'It would take hours. Might not even be possible. Some of that ground has to be solid rock.'

'I'm not big,' Tilly said. 'I could lean in with someone hanging on to my ankles.'

'And fall in on top of him and break your neck?' Harry shook his head. 'I'm not going to let that happen.'

'That's why I'd trust you to hang on to my ankles,' Tilly said. She was watching Harry intently and he found he couldn't look away from that gaze. From the trust he could see in her eyes. More than trust…?

The search and rescue team were talking behind them.

'It's not such a stupid idea. She's the only one here who's small enough to not get stuck in the shaft. If she was in a harness and roped in, we've got more than enough manpower to pull her out.

'I could get a harness on Sammy.' Tilly nodded.

'You'd be hanging upside down. It's not that easy to do anything.'

'But it's worth a try, isn't it?' Harry could see Tilly straightening her spine as she reached towards the harness one of the men was holding. 'Please? If there's any way we can get Sammy back to his nana quickly, we've got to try.'

Harry sensed the change around him. Because there were enough local people here who knew exactly why time was precious for the Grimshaw family. People who were prepared to break rules or protocols and do whatever they could to help. So he couldn't try and talk Tilly out of the idea. He could only watch her being buckled into a harness and ropes being attached with carabiners and instructions being given about how to attach another harness to Sammy.

And then he could only watch her being lowered into the hole, far enough for her feet to vanish from sight. He had to stand well back because nobody knew if there were ancient tunnels that could cause sinkholes if there was too much weight at ground level. Nobody knew how easily Tilly would be able to fit through the length of that shaft either, or what the effects might be on her body. Hanging upside down for more than a few minutes could lead to an increase in blood pressure and a decrease in heart rate. It could put pressure on the eyes and lead to blood pooling inside the head. It was possible that Tilly could pass out. It was also possible that her heart could stop when blood flow to her lower body was suddenly restored to a normal level.

She could die.

And it was that thought that made the breath catch in Harry's chest and made him close his eyes in pain as he realised just how much he didn't want that to happen. Not to this astonishingly courageous, beautiful, loving, *warm* woman he'd discovered Matilda Dawson to be.

He didn't want it to happen to someone he cared about *this* much...

He'd never been so relieved as he was in the moment, only minutes later, when Tilly was pulled back to safety. And, when it looked as if she might be about to faint when she tried to get up, he was the one who reached her first and held her steady in his arms.

'Don't move,' he told her. 'It's okay. I've got you...'

The pounding in Tilly's head was finally receding as little Sammy was carefully pulled out of the mineshaft and Harry was able to check him out physically and confirm that he was, miraculously, uninjured.

It was his father, John, who carried him off the hill and up to the homestead as the overjoyed volunteers began to pack up and go home to their own families—not before they'd shared a cup of tea and some Christmas baking, mind you.

Tilly found her father still behind the trestle table, pouring hot water into a large teapot.

'It's time you went home,' she told him.

'I'll wait a bit. You're going up to the house?'

'Yes. Just for a minute. Harry and I want to check on Maggie. She will have been through the wringer in the last few hours.'

Jim nodded. 'It's been a Christmas Eve to remember, that's for sure. Thank goodness we've had a happy ending.'

Tilly could see past the smile on her father's face. 'You're in a lot more pain, aren't you?'

'He's been on his feet too long,' Lizzie told her. 'I'm going to check that foot in a minute and, if necessary, I'll cart him off to hospital, don't you worry.'

Tilly smiled. 'Thanks, Lizzie. Might see you at home again a bit later?'

'Not likely, lovie.' Lizzie grinned back. 'It's almost midnight and at my age we all turn into pumpkins after that.'

By the time Tilly and Harry reached the

homestead and were welcomed inside, Sammy was cuddled up beside Maggie on her bed and nobody seemed at all bothered by the amount of dirt that had been spread on her sheets. George was snuggled under her nana's other arm. Tilly knelt by the head of the bed and Harry perched on the end. The rest of the family drifted further away, as if wanting to give Maggie privacy with her medical team. Sammy's mother called to her son.

'You hungry, Sammy? We've got cheese rolls that have just come out of the oven. They're your favourite.'

'Ooh, they sound good,' Harry said. 'What's a cheese roll?'

'South Island specialty,' Maggie told him. 'You'd better check that Tilly knows how to make them, Harry. It's at the top of the list for something a good southern wife should know how to make.'

Tilly jumped in to try and skate over the awkward moment. 'How are you feeling, Maggie? Can we do anything to help? How's that pain level?'

Tilly could see the way George snuggled even closer in beneath her grandmother's arm.

'It'll get better, Nana. That's what Santa said. It'll stop being sore.'

'It will, my darling girl,' Maggie said quietly. 'It will…'

Sammy also leaned closer. 'I'm sorry, Nana. I couldn't find Father Christmas to make our wish come true.'

'Some wishes aren't meant to come true, my love.' Maggie closed her eyes, her hand stroking Sammy's hair. 'But you know that part of me is never going to die, don't you?'

Sammy raised his head. 'What part, Nana?'

'The part that lives in here.' Maggie touched his chest. 'In your heart. It'll be there for ever. Even when I'm not here, you can talk to me whenever you want and, if you stay still and listen very carefully, you might even hear me say something back.'

Both George and Sammy were wide-eyed. They stared at their nana and then looked at each other. And smiled.

Tilly looked from the older woman and these beautiful children to the man sitting on the end of the bed. Not that she could see Harry very well because her eyes were filled with tears. But she could feel the tenderness of that smile and was quite sure that he was blinking back his own tears.

She could also feel her heart fill to bursting point again. Overflowing, in fact, as they all became aware of the faint sound drifting in through the open door of the house. A glance through the windows showed them that most of the horde of volunteers who had shown up to search for Sammy hadn't gone home just yet. Someone must have had the supply of candles that had been used for the carol service in the back of their ute and everybody was holding a tiny flame.

And they were all singing.

Silent night, holy night…

Tilly blinked away her tears and now she could see Harry's face with absolute clarity. And he was still smiling as he stood up and held out his hand.

'It's time we let Maggie rest,' he said. 'Let's go home, Tilly.'

CHAPTER ELEVEN

THE LYRICS OF the favourite carol were still in Tilly's head when they arrived home to a house that was completely dark apart from the twinkling coloured lights they could see through the big bay window of the living room.

'It's officially Christmas Day, Tilly.' Harry came around the car and opened the passenger door. 'Merry Christmas.'

Tilly had her phone in her hand. 'I've got a message from Lizzie. They've put Dad on complete bed rest in the ward and have his leg elevated to try and get the new swelling down. She'll give us an update when there's more news but says not to expect him home for Christmas dinner.'

'Oh, no… This wasn't part of the plan.'

Tilly tipped her head back against the seat and closed her eyes. 'No.'

None of it had been part of the plan, had it? She hadn't planned on her father hurting himself or Jason falling into a hay baler. She hadn't planned on Harry finding out her secret or discovering that maybe she'd really like to be a rural GP after all. Or having to go head-first down an abandoned mineshaft.

And she most definitely hadn't planned on falling in love with Harry Doyle.

It was officially Christmas Day. Which meant that tomorrow Harry would be flying back to the north island. Getting a step closer to tying up loose ends and heading back to his home in Ireland.

'Hey...' Harry's voice was soft and much closer to her ear than she might have expected. 'You still awake, Bat Woman?'

A smile curled the corners of Tilly's mouth. Harry hadn't wanted her to do that upside-down bat thing down the mineshaft, had he? But how proud of her had he looked when she came back up from the shaft having successfully attached the harness to Sammy? And, as for that smile when they'd been privileged enough to be part of that precious conversation between Maggie and her grandchildren...well...

Tilly didn't have time to finish that dreamy

thought because she felt one of Harry's arms slide behind her back and the other beneath her knees.

'I'm not surprised you're exhausted,' he said. 'Come on... I'm taking you to bed.'

*Oh...*there was a thought...

Tilly *was* exhausted. Emotionally as well as physically, so it wasn't that hard to quell any urge to restore her independence and walk inside by herself. Or to try and find any remnants of those protective barriers she'd relied on for so long and push Harry away. She didn't need to, anyway, because that unfinished thought had been about just how lucky you could be to have someone like Harry care about you. How much you could trust someone like him.

So Tilly simply wrapped her arms around Harry's neck and let him carry her into her bedroom. And when it felt as if he was about to put her down, she instinctively tightened that hold a little and lifted her face so that it became an invitation to be kissed. One that Harry seemed only too happy to accept.

And that kiss was so gentle. So tender that Tilly would have been only too happy to drown in it. She could feel herself sinking, in fact, but it turned out that Harry was just putting her down on her bed, without breaking the kiss. She could also feel the feather topping of her mattress creating the soft feeling of the interior of a nest and her pillow denting as it cradled her head. She could also feel the tension of Harry's muscles changing. He was really going to put her down this time, wasn't he?

'Don't go,' she whispered. 'Please…?'

'I wanted to find something. I have a Christmas gift for you, Tilly.'

The windows of Tilly's bedroom only looked out at her father's extensive vegetable garden but there was enough moonlight coming through them to be able to see Harry's face clearly. She couldn't see the blue of his eyes, but she could feel the intensity of his gaze and that it was just as tender as that kiss had been. She held on to it as she gathered possibly the most courage she'd ever needed in her life.

'You don't need to go anywhere to give me what my wish is for this Christmas.'

He knew.

He knew that Tilly felt safe enough to ask him for something she could never ask of anyone else. A chance to find out if she could get past the damage that had been done to both her mind and body. It could only ever be Harry who could give her that gift because he was the one who'd given her the confidence to see the real truth and she knew, deep in her soul, that he had the kindness and patience to make it safe. Even if this time together, away from the only reality they'd previously known, would be over in no more than a matter of hours, he had the power to change her whole life.

To help her become a person she could be proud of being…

The touch of Harry's fingers as they traced the outline of her face was as gentle as everything else about this man.

'You're so tired, sweetheart… Are you sure?'

Was she sure? Even though it was highly likely that this would increase the heartbreak that was rushing towards her like an emotional freight train?

Yes, she was sure. Maybe partly because of that impending heartbreak, even. Because it meant she could feel this kind of desire. This level of love. This fierce need to be this close to Harry that was a heat that melted every other thought as his lips claimed hers again.

Perhaps the exhaustion actually helped to make this the perfect time, allowing Tilly's body to go with the gentle flow of Harry's lovemaking and avoid any subconscious urge to back away into any familiar, safe space. It was Tilly who begged for more in the end, welcoming the most intimate touch of all with her arms wrapped so tightly around this man she loved that she couldn't quite tell where her body ended and his began. And that only made it even more perfect.

It was the heat that finally woke Harry.

In that first heartbeat of consciousness he was aware of several things. The softness of Tilly's body curled against his, with her breath a puff of extra warmth on his skin. The tingle of his own body that wanted to remind him of everything that had happened right up until the birds were announcing the imminent arrival of dawn—not that he was likely to forget a single moment of the most astonishingly memorable sex he'd ever experienced.

He was also aware that it was Christmas Day. That there was blazing sunshine outside already and it would probably be even hotter than yesterday. And he was realising that the sunshine and heat didn't feel so wrong now. It didn't make it feel any less like Christmas.

Real Christmas had very little to do with places or weather. It was about people and the connections between them, wasn't it? The kind of joy a baby's birth had brought centuries ago. The peace that someone could bestow on her beloved grandchildren as a final gift. The community spirit that could bring so many people together, not only to find a lost little boy, but to celebrate by staying together and using a Christmas song to share that connection. And, okay, it might be about showing how much you cared by giving things to others, but some things couldn't be wrapped—couldn't be seen, even—but they could potentially be the most precious gifts ever bestowed.

Like the gift that he and Tilly had shared during the earliest hours of this Christmas Day. The gift of trust. Of passion. Of a love that would be there for ever, even if they ended up a world apart.

Harry bent his head and pressed a kiss onto Tilly's hair. Just a soft touch but it was enough to make her eyelashes flutter and then lift to reveal her eyes. Harry was so glad he'd woken first because that meant he could see the moment that Tilly became aware of a whole lot of things, just like he had, and he could see that she was as happy as he was. That this had to be the best Christmas morning ever.

'Hey…' Harry whispered. 'Merry Christmas, Bat Woman.'

'Merry Christmas, Leprechaun Man.'

'Shall I get up and make us some coffee?'

'Not just yet.' Tilly brushed her lips against his skin, closing her eyes. 'I want to make sure I remember the dream I had about you.'

Harry could feel the rumble of his soft laughter as he pulled Tilly closer. 'It was no dream. I was there too, remember?'

Tilly's eyes opened. 'I've got a gift for you.'

'I think you already gave it to me.'

The flush of colour in her cheeks was a delight. 'No…this is something you can take back to Ireland with you. Oh…' Her eyes widened. 'What time is it? I should probably have put the turkey in the oven hours ago. And I have to look up a recipe for bread sauce and pick a whole bucket of peas from the garden.'

But Harry shook his head. 'The food is

like snow,' he said. 'It's not the thing that makes it really Christmas.'

There was a question in Tilly's eyes.

'This is,' he added. 'Family. Friends. Feeling like you're home…' Then he smiled. 'There is one thing that I'd really like for Christmas dinner, mind. And I don't think it'll take too long.'

'What's that?'

'That potato thing. The one my mammy used to make for me.'

'Potato gratin.' Tilly was smiling back at him. 'I think I can manage that.'

Harry leaned down to kiss her. 'Let's do it together.'

It was easy enough to find a recipe online and, as luck would have it, they had all the ingredients they needed and plenty of time before they were planning to go and visit Jim in the hospital and take him his Christmas gifts.

They sliced potatoes very thinly and layered them with the butter and cream and garlic they'd melted, sprinkling in salt and pepper, thyme and Gruyère cheese. They baked it until it was golden and bubbly on top and crispy and brown around the edges and, when it had cooled just enough, they ate it, sitting outside in the shady courtyard—in the space where Harry had kissed Tilly for the very first time.

'This is the best Christmas dinner I've ever had,' Harry announced.

Tilly thought so too, but that wasn't only because of the food. Like Harry had said, this was about the company she had and the connection she was never going to lose with the man who had given her the gift of a new life.

'Are you going to open your present now?'

'Are you going to open yours?'

The two small boxes were sitting on the table, looking remarkably similar apart from their colour.

'Wouldn't it be funny if we've given each other exactly the same thing?' Tilly reached for the silver box.

'It would.' Harry picked up the green box.

They opened them together and Tilly stared at the intricate silver design of the necklace nestled on rumpled silk. Harry was blinking at a greenstone pendant with a rustic string cord.

'It's a koru,' Tilly told him. 'It's a Maori design based on the unfurling bit of a new fern frond. It represents creation. A new life but also coming back to a beginning—a point of origin. It made me think of you going home to Ireland and finding the new life where you belong, at home.'

She could see the movement of Harry's throat as he swallowed. 'And yours is a Celtic symbol. A Dara Knot, which symbolises strength and courage. The kind you've got. The kind that you can use to find the new life that you deserve.'

Tilly could feel the tears gathering in her eyes as she picked up the beautiful piece of jewellery. 'We *have* given each other the same thing.'

'Except I'm not sure I want to find my new life in Ireland.' Harry was holding the smooth greenstone carving in his hand. 'I'm not sure it's going to feel enough like home any longer.'

'Why not?'

'Because you won't be there.'

'I could be,' Tilly whispered. 'If you wanted me to be?'

But Harry shook his head. 'You belong here,' he said. 'I've only been here for two days but I can see that this is your home. You have family here. A whole community that you belong to.'

'But maybe this won't feel completely like home for me now, either.'

Oh...the blue of Harry's eyes had never been so intense. 'Is that because I wouldn't be here?'

'I think it might be.'

'I like it here,' Harry said slowly. 'I'd like to visit Ireland again, of course, but I think I could live here. Possibly for ever.'

Tilly drew in a shaky breath. In real terms, she and Harry had only just met. There was no way they could know what the future held or whether how they felt about each other could grow into something permanent and precious. But even for ever had to start somewhere, didn't it?

With a moment, just like this…?

Her smile wobbled. 'For ever is quite a long time, you know.'

Harry's smile didn't wobble at all. 'I know…'

EPILOGUE

Five years later...

'Mumma?'

'Yes, darling?'

'There's *boots*. Like Dadda's.' Three-year-old Maggie was very excited, leaning forward so that it was impossible for her father to do up the buckle of her car seat harness. *'Look...'*

Tilly looked. She didn't need her daughter to be pointing at the roof of the old villa to know that Harry had done what he'd sworn he'd never do. He'd climbed up onto the roof and put Santa's legs into the chimney with his feet sticking out. And wee Maggie thought it was as hilarious as Tilly had when she'd been a small child. She was beside herself with mirth as Harry finally did up the buckle.

'He's up-down, Dadda. He's stuck...'

'Your Mammy's good at being upside down too, sweetheart. But she didn't get stuck, thank goodness...' He winked at Tilly, reaching out to take the plastic container full of cheese rolls—their contribution to the Craig's Gully Christmas Eve community barbecue—from her hands.

'I'd get stuck now,' she said. 'I might get stuck even if I'm not up-down.'

Harry eyed the impressive bump of her belly and his smile widened. 'You might, to be fair... I know I said I wanted six kids, but they don't have to all come at once.'

'It's only twins.'

Harry held the door open so that Tilly could climb into the truck. Then he leaned in to kiss her. 'I'm just going to check on... you know...'

'I know...'

'Where's Dadda gone?'

'He'll be back in a minute, darling. Shall we listen to a song while we wait?' Tilly opened her Christmas folder and put the music through the car's speakers. A New Zealand version of a carol that was a family favourite, that had one of the three Kings of the Orient in a tractor and another in a car.

She watched Harry disappear into the

barn. He'd be checking that her father had finished getting into the Father Christmas suit and that Lizzie was all set to drive him down to the town square. Tilly smiled. Her father had grown a beard himself in the last couple of years, so he was beginning to look rather like Father Christmas even without the costume.

A perfect grandfather.

And an amazing father, as always. His wedding gift to Harry and Tilly, only six months after he'd first met his potential son-in-law that Christmas, had been to sign over the old family homestead to them. He needed a smaller place in town, he'd said. A place that Lizzie could help him choose because it looked like they were set to keep each other company for the rest of their lives.

That first year had been so busy for all of them with a wedding to plan and living and work arrangements to update. It had only got busier since then but none of them were complaining. Tilly hadn't ended up taking over the family practice from her father, but who would have guessed that a job in the emergency department of their local hospital would have opened up? Or that Harry would embrace getting the qualifications to become a GP and to join a bigger practice that gave him time to be a popular local doctor, a very hands-on father and even a member of the mountain search and rescue team?

With the support team, including Jim and Lizzie and offers of local help streaming in ever since the news of the twins' arrival had spread like wildfire, Tilly knew exactly how lucky she was to have the career she loved so much and now the joy of a family she'd never dreamed of having.

The chorus of the song was coming on again and Maggie was singing along about the king on his scooter...tooting his hooter... with far more enthusiasm than tunefulness. A glance in the rear-view mirror showed Tilly that her father, in the Santa suit, was climbing into Lizzie's car and Harry was carefully closing the door of the barn behind them. Maggie might realise that it was her grandpa who was hearing her secret wish for Christmas this year, but she would have no idea that the magic had already happened.

Pudding was being hidden in the barn until tomorrow morning. How lucky was it that Jason's children had outgrown the bombproof little palomino pony just as Maggie was ready for more than simply sitting on Spud, who was still enjoying life but really only wanted to stand in the shade of the nearest tree.

Tilly could do with the shade of a tree to sit under right now. It was going to be another hot Christmas Day tomorrow and maybe they could take Maggie to the lake in the afternoon for a swim. After they'd done the whole traditional Christmas dinner thing, of course. Lizzie was coming early to help with all the cooking, but Tilly and Harry had already prepared their favourite part of the feast and the baking dish filled with potato gratin was in the fridge, all ready for the oven.

She could see Harry striding back towards the car now. He was close enough for Tilly to see the way he looked up at the roof of the house and she could see the grin that advertised how pleased he was with reinstating another Christmas tradition. Her love for the man she had married was a huge squeeze around her heart that never failed to take her breath away.

He'd be sneaking off to climb the roof and put the Santa legs in the chimney every year from now on, wouldn't he?

For ever.

Tilly was smiling at Harry as he climbed into the driving seat. A misty kind of smile that came from a place of pure joy.

How lucky was she that for ever was such a long time?

* * * * *

*If you enjoyed this story, check out
these other great reads from
Alison Roberts*

One Weekend in Prague
A Paramedic to Change Her Life
Miracle Baby, Miracle Family
The Vet's Unexpected Family

All available now!